PRAISE FO
DOROTHY SALISBURY DAVIS

"Dashiell Hammett, Raymond Chandler and Josephine Tey . . . Dorothy Salisbury Davis belongs in the same company. She writes with great insight into the psychological motivations of all her characters." —*The Denver Post*

"Dorothy Salisbury Davis may very well be the best mystery novelist around." —*The Miami Herald*

"Davis has few equals in setting up a puzzle, complete with misdirection and surprises." —*The New York Times Book Review*

"Davis is one of the truly distinguished writers in the medium; what may be more important, she is one of the few who can build suspense to a sonic peak." —Dorothy B. Hughes, *Los Angeles Times*

"A joyous and unqualified success." —*The New York Times* on *Death of an Old Sinner*

"An intelligent, well-written thriller." —*Daily Mirror* on *Death of an Old Sinner*

"At once gentle and suspenseful, warmly humorous and tensely perplexing." —*The New York Times* on *A Gentleman Called*

"Superbly developed, gruesomely upsetting." —*Chicago Tribune* on *A Gentleman Called*

"An excellent, well-controlled piece of work." —*The New Yorker* on *The Judas Cat*

"A book to be long remembered." —*St. Louis Post-Dispatch* on *A Town of Masks*

"Mrs. Davis has belied the old publishing saying that an author's second novel is usually less good than the first. Since her first ranked among last year's best, what more need be said?" —*The New York Times* on *The Clay Hand*

"Ingeniously plotted . . . A story of a young woman discovering what is real in life and in herself." —*The New York Times* on *A Death in the Life*

"Davis brings together all the elements needed for a good suspense story to make this, her fourth Julie Hayes, her best." —*Library Journal* on *The Habit of Fear*

"Mrs. Davis is one of the admired writers of American mystery fiction, and *Shock Wave* is up to her best. She has a cultured style, handles dialogue with a sure ear, and understands people better than most of her colleagues." —*The New York Times Book Review* on *Shock Wave*

OLD
SINNERS
NEVER DIE

OLD
SINNERS
NEVER DIE

A Mrs. Norris Mystery

DOROTHY SALISBURY DAVIS

OPEN ROAD

INTEGRATED MEDIA

NEW YORK

Cover design by Tracey Dunham

ISBN 978-1-4804-6043-0

This edition published in 2014 by Open Road Integrated Media, Inc.
345 Hudson Street
New York, NY 10014
www.openroadmedia.com

PREFACE

General Jarvis is dead, of course. The extraordinary finish to a life that was itself rarely ordinary was accounted in *Death of an Old Sinner*. So many people have been kind enough to say that he died too soon—I pass over the dissenters, certain of them within his own household—that I now propose to tell a tale of him when he was a younger man, short of seventy. For his part in this escapade I am guided by the late General's notes for his memoirs. Alas, those memoirs were never finished, his having got on with the publisher's advance of several thousand dollars so much faster than with the writing of the book. Also, every time he took pen in hand, he suffered from what might be called intimations of libel. Therefore, let me say forthwith, all the characters herein are fictional; and this includes the General.

DSD

OLD
SINNERS
NEVER DIE

1

There are seasons in Washington when it is even more difficult than usual to find out what is going on in the government. Possibly this is because nothing is going on, although a great many people seem to be working at it. Such a season occurs during the first months of change in presidential administrations. An army of newcomers is then engaged in finding places. For themselves, of course: boldly, shamelessly, ruthlessly. This is refreshing: it only becomes sordid when they start looking for places for others. The old-timers who survive the season engage themselves for its duration almost entirely in the culling of retirement lists.

So ran the speculation of Major General Ransom Jarvis on that spring afternoon in 1953 when he was put on notice that his own retirement was imminent. The General's blast of wrath all but trembled the Pentagon. Then the old boy went home for the day. He loathed his desk anyway, and it was there he had been tethered since the war's end in Europe. But it was going to be a great deal more loathsome to get along on retirement pay. A man's income should be doubled, not halved, to match the time he was given to spend it in the last, numbered years of his life.

Among the varied oppressions settling on the General as afternoon advanced into evening was a sense of parsimony. He lived at his club; he had never before quibbled with his conscience over what he put on his bar bill, but that was the state in which he now found himself. It was natural, therefore, that his thoughts turned to the presence in Washington of his son, James. Jimmie was the freshman representative from a congressional district the number of which Ransom Jarvis never could remember although he had maintained his family residence there all the years of his life. It was there, he supposed, he would have to go on retirement—to the dour care of a Scotch housekeeper who had got her start in America as nursemaid to his son! Damn it, he had not lived that long. Certainly, not that much. About to motion the bartender, his thoughts turned again to Jimmie, or more specifically, to the twelve-year-old Scotch whisky he was sure the boy favoured in Washington as well as at home. He forewent a second drink at the bar.

Whatever kind of a son Jimmie had been in other ways, he prided himself on the patience with which he had always lis-

4

tened to his father. Considering the worth of that gentleman's advice over the years, such patience was by now heroic. And that afternoon he was hard put. As a dear friend had said slyly after her congratulatory kiss on his election, he was now to have the winning candidate's just reward: the privilege of listening to the speeches of all the other winning candidates in the country. That was the kind of day it had been.

"But it shouldn't have happened to me during this—of all—administrations," the General complained of his retirement notice.

"You are well into your sixties, aren't you, Father? If it hadn't been for Korea this would have happened some time ago."

"I'm in my prime, boy! I could have run for president myself. Sound as a hound dog's tooth."

"The word is 'clean'. Clean as a hound dog's tooth," Jimmie said patiently.

The General grunted. "Huh. That's something else again, isn't it?"

Jimmie grinned and poured them both another drink.

His father looked about, wondering if he had not been in this house before at, say, an affair of some now extinct embassy or such. Newly decorated, of course. There were two smells he always associated with Washington. One was fresh paint. "Isn't this place a little large for you, Jimmie?"

"No."

"Are they paying congressmen this much salary these days?"

"No."

The General tried another tack. "The club has always

5

suited me when I've been stateside. I'm limited, of course, in the entertaining I can do there—so to speak."

Jimmie grinned. "So to speak, I am too, Father."

"I wasn't speaking of that kind of entertainment. When a man reaches my age, he needs friends . . ."

Oh, Lord, Jimmie thought, and once more lamented the event that had brought him to Washington and a father's care.

"He needs friends," the old man repeated sententiously, and then looked up. "Or money."

"I suppose you're going to have to face up to that aspect of it," Jimmie said blandly.

"Somebody is, and I don't think it's going to be the United States government!"

Jimmie took a long pull at his drink. "Would you like to move in here with me, Father?"

"Not if I can help it."

Jimmie laughed—out of gratification as much as amusement at the old man's bluntness. "We could bring Mrs. Norris down and live like a proper family, God help us."

Then Ransom Jarvis, surprising himself almost as much as he did Jimmie, said, "I suppose we might try it for a while." He was prompted by several considerations: if he were going to have eventually to retire to the care of Mrs. Norris, he might as well get used to it here before settling into isolation with her in the old house on the Hudson River; and he could save money living on Jimmie, as it were. He would make an occasional gesture, of course, but Jimmie had inherited entirely from his mother, and it the fortune he—Ransom Jarvis—had married into. All in all, he had not done very well by himself in such arrangements, for ultimately he also must take credit for having hired Mrs. Norris and, therefore, for the careful training she had given his son with regard to money. There was not a bairn raised in Scotland with a tighter fist than his son James.

"Do you mean it, Father?"

"Of course I mean it. Since you've taken the precaution of making a home, we should . . . sanctify it."

"It was not a precaution," Jimmie said. "I like a home, I am conservative by nature."

"Mmm. Not by your father's nature. By your mother's, I dare say. And Mrs. Norris'. She puts up a good argument for environment. Her kind always does, God help me."

Jimmie laughed in spite of himself and looked the old gentleman up and down. He really was in the prime, limber of brain and joint, and bristling with energy. Jimmie drew a deep breath and said, "We must have been switched in our cradles, Father."

The General was pleased. His glass in hand, he made a tour of the house. The neighbourhood was good: Georgetown, after all. And his son's tastes were to his own liking. There was a smell of leather in the study, well-bound books, good light . . . He conjured the picture of himself at work there on his own memoirs. There ought to be something in the past he could turn into a contemporary dollar—by means other than blackmail. Such was the turn his mind took with his first glimpse at the more interesting aspects of his career. He would have to be careful what he said about some people in high places, considering what he thought of them, though damn few people high or low were careful what they said about him.

He paused at a piece of sculpture and ran his hand over it, a vivid bronze nude. "Helene's work?"

Jimmie nodded. His father's reference was to Jimmie's friend, Helene Joyce, a sculptress, whose work was beginning to get international notice.

"I'll be able to sit for her now," the General said. "She's been wanting to do me, you know. Admires my head. Viewing it from the outside, that is. Let me know when she comes to Washington."

Jimmie said, "I think I might put through a call to Mrs. Norris now."

The General gave a great bark of laughter, and that made him realize that his humour had much improved. "I'll go along then, Jimmie, and start to pack."

"I've got an extra pair of pyjamas," Jimmie said dryly.

His father chose to take the words at their literal value. "Thank you, my boy, but I want to get used to the idea gradually. I've not had the offer of such hospitality since the Russians in Berlin."

Jimmie went to the door with him. "I wouldn't tell that story as much abroad as I used to if I were you, Father."

"Eh? What story's that?"

"About how well you got on with the Russians."

"Don't tell me I'm getting to be a bore with it?"

"That wasn't what I meant."

The old gentleman shaped his soft hat and put it on carefully. "Curious, how often we can stand hearing ourselves tell the same story, and go stark mad at the repetition of someone else. I promise I'll watch myself, boy."

"We'll devise a set of signals," Jimmie said. "Good-night, Father."

The General turned around at the door. "I don't think we should start off being too damned congenial. Let's leave a bit of open ground between us, so we can improve our positions, shall we?"

It was amazing, Jimmie thought, contemplating his affairs in the wake of his father's visit, how complicated a man's life could become despite his best efforts to keep it simple. One would suppose, for example, that his remaining a bachelor would ensure no household entanglements. But here he was, having suddenly to reorganize a whole ménage. He had no business bringing Mrs. Norris to Washington at all; so much of his time would have to be spent among his constituents, at home she quite belonged there. But without her, frankly, he did not think he could cope with his father, especially in this hour of the old man's discontent.

How, he wondered, was Mrs. Norris going to take to Tom Hennessy? Hennessy was a young man no farther from Ireland than his first citizenship papers, a natural-born politician, a lad with good looks and talent and far more political ambition than the man who had hired him. He was in the kitchen now, studying the finer points of parliamentarianism in case Jimmie had occasion to consult him. He was, if Jimmie had to give a name to his position, a sort of chauffeur-valet, although Jimmie had overheard him once (on the telephone) identify himself as "the congressman's press secretary".

Jimmie decided to speak to him now about Mrs. Norris.

"Sure, we'll get along fine, sir, as long as she's older than me. If it was a young one you were bringing in now . . ."

"God forbid," Jimmie said.

"It'll be simple," Tom said. "I'll do for you and she'll do for me."

"It's the General we shall all have to look out for," Jimmie said, knowing very well that Mrs. Norris would soon teach young Tom who was going to do for whom.

"He's a bit lively for his age, is he?"

"Yes," Jimmie said quietly, "I guess that's as good a word for it as any."

2

Two days after Jimmie's call, Mrs. Norris managed to reach Washington. The General had already moved in. It was a day that all of them expected would be busy. And the night promised to be busy also, and very gay, for it was the occasion of the Beaux Arts Ball. But no one had any notion at all of just how busy their next twenty-four hours was to be.

Mrs. Norris arrived by early train. There was nothing she liked better than to be sent for. She was, therefore, slightly put out that Mr. James was not able to meet her himself. He had always managed it, no matter how busy, on other occasions. She looked up at the tall young man who gathered both her bags from her scarcely a moment after she stepped from the carriage.

"I'm Tom Hennessy, ma'am," he said with a smile that opened his face on a beautiful set of teeth. "I'm Mr. Jarvis' personal."

"His personal what?"

"He'll have to tell you that himself, Mrs. Norris, for he hasn't made up his mind yet."

Mrs. Norris allowed herself to be led into and through the station and out to the car. Mr. James had sent that for her anyway. "How did you know me?"

"Mr. Jarvis described you—pert and perky," the young man said with more tact than she'd ordinarily have credited the Irish.

"I'll give odds it was my hat he described."

"He might have mentioned it," the young man said, throwing open the back door of the car to her. "But we're awful glad, all of us here, to see it tossed into the ring."

"I'll ride in the front seat with you," Mrs. Norris said, giving an authoritative nod of her head, and unsmiling. She had no intention of committing herself on first acquaintance to any man, be he squire or servant, youth or dotard.

3

Congressman Jarvis was at that moment as happily engaged as he was ever likely to be in the line of duty. Amongst the obscure committees to which he, a freshman in the House, might have been assigned was one on parks and monuments. Jimmie drew a seat on it, perhaps because in that particular session he was one of the few men in Congress able to distinguish between Pocahontas and Venus de Milo. It was altogether within the province of his office, therefore, that he met the plane on which Helene Joyce arrived in Washington that morning. Very briefly, he toyed with the notion of striped trousers and morning coat. But one never knew what he was likely to be requisitioned into at the airport in that guise.

Helene came down the ramp, a lovely mixture of furs and smiles, a hand extended, Jimmie thought to him, but just as she touched foot to ground, a gentleman in striped trousers stepped forward and caught the outstretched hand, lifted it to his lips, and showed no inclination to let it go. Helene's eyes were dancing with mischief.

"Jimmie, how nice to see you!" she cried, peering over the stranger's shoulder, and quite as though she had come on him by chance instead of arrangement. "May I present Dr. Henri d'Inde of the National Museum?"

Dr. d'Inde turned and clicked his heels, a French Impressionist no doubt, Jimmie thought glumly. Helene said, "Representative James Jarvis, Doctor."

D'Inde smiled optimistically. "Ahha! Your congressman, Madame, no?"

"Only in a manner of speaking, Doctor," Helene said in that deep-throated, sensuous tone that touched Jimmie to the marrow, and disengaging her one hand from the doctor's, she gave it and her other to Jimmie. Everything was going to be just fine.

"My dear, you look wonderful," she said and kissed his cheek. "Those campaign circles are gone from under your eyes."

"I have no trouble sleeping now," he said, "night or day. In fact, I have trouble in the daytime keeping awake."

Helene laughed.

"May we drop you somewhere, Congressman?" the museum man asked.

Jimmie assumed he had some such place as the Potomac River in mind, but he smiled and said, "I was about to ask you the same thing, Doctor."

Helene intervened, "Dr. d'Inde, I had no idea you would do me this honour, so I'd asked Jimmie to meet me, you see. Would you mind very much if I were just to come in to your office later this morning?"

"But, of course, Madame Joyce," he said pleasantly, again bowing.

He was the sort, Jimmie thought, who could turn a moment's gallantry into a lifetime advantage.

"He boasts of having seven children," Helene said placatingly as d'Inde took his departure. "He's a family man."

"I should hope so, with seven children," Jimmie said.

"I think he's very good looking, don't you?"

"Exquisite," Jimmie said.

"I'm touched even if you're pretending," Helene said, and laid her hand on his arm. "Aren't you proud of me to have got the commission? That's why d'Inde came to meet me, you know."

Jimmie squeezed her hand against him. "I'm very proud, and more than that, dear." He gave her luggage ticket to a porter, and asked for a cab. To Helene he said, "Mrs. Norris comes down by train this morning. With her here you could have been our house guest quite decently."

"The old hotel is better for me, but thank you, Jimmie."

"Likely you're right. Father's decided to move in with me now."

"Oh, dear. Your life is complicated."

"All I need is a wife," Jimmie said slyly.

"And what would Mrs. Norris do then, poor thing?"

"You two have never met, have you?"

"No, but I agree, Jimmie. Discretion is the better part of valour. Will you excuse me a moment, dear? There's a hat box I want to make sure our man doesn't miss."

She had a great habit of agreeing with him on something he hadn't said whenever he brought the subject of matrimony anywhere near the conversation, thereby deflecting him while making it seem he had saved himself. Helene had been married very young—in her Greenwich Village days, the days when she was herself a student of sculpture and a model—and the marriage had smashed very soon and very painfully for her whether by death, annulment, or possibly desertion: Jimmie had heard rumours of all of them, and considerably more of gossip about Mrs. Joyce. But even if she did some day consent to marry him, Jimmie was the sort who would not pry beyond her wish to confide. She had once said of him, he was far too tolerant for a man with political ambition. They had met only a few years ago at Helene's first major exhibition. Now she had fame. She wore it quite as well as the beauty she had preserved through a youth of struggle. She must be about his own age, Jimmie thought, the late thirties, and if she were an example of what came out of the school of hard knocks, he might wish he had had a scholarship to it himself.

In the car riding along Massachusetts Avenue, Jimmie said,

"I hope that dandy d'Inde hasn't planned to take you to the Beaux Arts Ball."

"Isn't it wonderful that there's to be a Beaux Arts Ball in Washington?" Helene again diverted him. "I'm very pleased to have been asked."

"Without you there could be no Arts Ball—for me anyway," he said.

Helene cast him a sidelong glance; her expression was one of amused affection. "It must be a dreadful chore to have to make up the guest list for such affairs, everybody expecting to be invited."

"You would be surprised how many in this town won't risk being seen at affairs like this just now."

"You *are* joking, Jimmie?"

"Not entirely. I'll tell you this, Helene: there will be people there tonight keeping careful watch to see whom other people talk to."

"Aren't there always at such functions?" she said lightly.

"Yes, but the possibilities have rarely been so lethal."

She looked at him. "Politically, you mean?"

He nodded. "And in Washington. Therefore, economically, socially."

She sat in silence a moment, thinking. "Do you plan to do anything about it—in Congress?"

"What can I do? I'm a freshman—too young, except to vote."

"And are all the rest too old?"

Jimmie said nothing. He did not like what was called "the

temper of the times" or "the climate of Washington" in that year of 1953, and he was well aware that his own background of conservatism all but delivered him from inquisition. It was a situation for which he felt very nearly apologetic among friends like Helene.

"Wouldn't it have been a fine idea," she said, deliberately trying to be light about it now, "to have made the ball a masquerade? Then everyone might have been safe talking to anybody."

"It was planned that way actually," Jimmie answered. "Then Senator Fagan inquired why. 'Why a masquerade?' he said. 'What are you trying to pull?'."

"And that's why you changed it," Helene said incredulously, "because he inquired?"

"It was thought better by the committee," Jimmie said carefully, "that none of us seem to hide our faces from him." Even as he told it he realized the fallacy of the position: they, the committee of which he was a member, had thought themselves quite brave in the decision; what now seemed apparent was their self-deception: all they had done was mask their capitulation to the senator.

Helene drew up the collar of her fur jacket and yet it was a warm spring day. "Is it too early for you to have a drink, Jimmie?"

"No, though I'd prefer it not in a public place."

"I've taken a suite," she said. "It will be all right there."

"So I understand," he said, "that you have a suite."

"I thought I should have a parlour into which I might

invite you. Also, I've arranged to show some of my work—a few pieces to some special people."

"Like dandy d'Inde, I suppose."

"You're being ridiculous, Jimmie, and just a little nasty."

"I feel nasty. Weren't you touched by his turning out to meet you in striped trousers?"

"Amused slightly. But rather shaken that an artist should take the time to go in for such nonsense."

Jimmie mumbled a guilty agreement, and felt even nastier, but with himself.

4

Mrs. Norris approved of the house, a three-storey brick building, Georgian, and modernized by a woman, she decided. She was to have more of a staff here than at home: a cook and a cleaning woman, a laundress, and whatever the Irishman called himself, she had chosen to make him a butler. He was a willing student, not, she soon discovered, because he fancied himself serving at table, but because he fancied himself sitting at table and wanted to know as much of what to do with "the instruments" as he could learn as a butler.

"It will take more than a ken of the instruments, my lad, to make you musical," Mrs. Norris advised on the afternoon of her arrival.

"You know, m'lady, your coming will bring me a devil of

a lot more work into the house," Hennessy said finally, having failed in twenty ways of trying to please her throughout the day.

"It'd be a great pity to see you idle when it takes no more to keep you in work. Have you laid out Mr. James' clothes for the evening?"

"I have. And his batman is up doing the same for the old gentleman now."

"Batman," Mrs. Norris repeated. "I haven't heard that word since the old country. They call them something else here."

"Orderly. M'lorderly's orderly. That takes a twist of the tongue, don't it?" Hennessy sat down and watched Mrs. Norris where she was inspecting the silver he had polished. "Don't you wish you were going to the ball tonight? What'ud a fella have to do to get invited, d'you suppose, if he wasn't elected to something? I wrote a few poems once to a girl. That'd be art enough, wouldn't it?"

"Did you have them put in a book?" Mrs. Norris asked, liking a bit of romantic verse now and then herself.

"Her father burned most of them, bad luck to him, but I rescued a few. Would you like to see them?"

"I would, some time."

"I'll fetch them right now and you can read them at leisure."

He was off at a gallop and soon was back with a well-thumbed envelope. "I can recite them if you like and save your eyesight."

"I've nothing better to save it for," she said, and tucked the envelope into the pocket of her second-best dress which she was still wearing beneath the tea apron.

Tom ran his tongue around his lips. "There's one I call 'Never sally if you can dally'."

"Tom, you're a villain," she said, looking at him out of the corner of her eye. He was very handsome.

"Well, I work part time at it," he said, and grinned.

"You worked part time at this, too," she said, giving him a serving fork to polish over.

"Would you know this Mrs. Joyce the boss is taking to the ball tonight?"

"I do and I don't," she said, not wanting to admit to him she had never met the woman.

"She's a fine looker, she is—lean as a colt, and I'll bet she could lead a man a wild chase."

"You've not the right to be talking like that, shame," Mrs. Norris said, burring the "r" in "right". "And when did you see her?"

"When I took round the flowers for himself a while ago."

"You were supposed to have them sent."

"Aw, you can't depend on the delivery service on a day like this, Mrs. Norris. I wasn't going to take any chance on them never arriving."

"You're a villain true, and I hope Mr. James puts you in your place before you're too big for it."

"I'm glad I went around all the same," Tom said. "The boss isn't the only one she has on the string."

"No?" Mrs. Norris said, wanting to keep him going without encouraging him.

"There was some French fella there just waiting to see my heels. But she wasn't in any hurry to push me out, I'll say that for her. Or maybe it's for myself I should say it. You know, she introduced me—me, mind you—to this Frenchman. I wish I could think of his name. It's something that rhymes with Dan, but not quite. My father's name was Dan, God rest him."

"She wanted you to carry the tale home, that's all," Mrs. Norris said.

"To make the boss jealous?"

"I wouldn't say just that," Mrs. Norris said, "but after all, Mr. James is a man of many interests, too."

Tom squinted up at her. "Is he now? You wouldn't be jealous yourself in your fashion?"

"I would not. You'll have the pattern rubbed off the fork there. Give it to me."

And at that moment a sudden blast of wind flushed the curtains, the drapes, Mrs. Norris' apron and hair, and a great booming voice hallooed through the house.

"The General is home," she said. "I must wash my hands."

But he was into the pantry before she could more than wipe them in her apron. "Well, and how's my bonnie lass?" he cried.

Mrs. Norris gave a bob of a curtsey. "I'm fine, sir thank you, and you look very well if I may say so."

He nodded, smiling, and began removing the buckles from his blouse. "By God, it's nice to be in a house that's a home," he said.

Tom snickered, and the General glanced round at him. "Did you speak?"

23

"No, sir. I was breathing."

"Then go out and breathe in the kitchen. I want to talk to Mrs. Norris." When the young man was gone, he said, "Shall we conspire against him, you and I? The place is so damned cluttered with help you can't say a word. Well, I daresay you could handle a regiment, and it's none of my business. We'll have a drink, shall we? Does he keep a decent bottle in the pantry?"

"If he does, he won't for long," Mrs. Norris said. "I'll see to that."

"Ah-ha! That fellow's Irish, isn't he?" the General said, finding a bottle of whisky and two glasses.

"But do you know, sir, he doesn't drink? He's taken the pledge."

The General grunted. "Sometimes I think there's something to what they say about this damned bomb turning the world inside out. Think of that: an Irishman who doesn't drink." He lifted his glass. "Cheers, old girl."

"Your health, sir, and your happiness." Mrs. Norris took her whisky as neat as did the General, but not so often.

"Happiness," the General repeated morosely. "Well, I'll go up and have my bath and a bit of a nap before dressing. You and I will have to renew our acquaintanceship. They're retiring me soon, you know. It will be into your custody probably."

"God ha' mercy, sir!" she clapped her hand to her mouth. It was the drink that spoke, not she.

The General laughed and went to the door. "Is it true, Mrs. Joyce is down for the ball?"

"I understand she is, sir."

"Do you know he never let on to me she was coming? Well. That makes me feel better at least, he's afraid of my competition."

"Are you going with someone important yourself, sir?"

The General peered into her face. "Whomever I go with shall be important, Mrs. Norris."

The arrogant old sinner, Mrs. Norris thought. All the same, there was something about him that could charm the heart of a wheelbarrow.

5

A great many dinner parties preceded the Arts Ball. One of the better-kept secrets of Washington was the manner in which hostesses on such occasions arrived at a fair and equitable distribution of very important people, important people, and people who had to be invited because they were important to the very important people.

It was a fine art in itself, the General thought, shaking hands with his host, to pair off an ageing stag like himself with someone it was hoped he might see to the ball after-wards. Ed Chatterton, an under secretary of state, was an old friend of the General's, a career diplomat. With a wealthy wife, he mused, observing the gold plate as he passed the dining room door on his way to the study. There were damn few posts in the service of the United States government to which a wealthy wife was not a man's very great asset. Fancy that: a man's patriotic duty to marry money! Hurrah for democracy!

In the study where the drinks were set out, the General found two gentlemen in the interesting position of examining the labels on the bottles without disturbing the bottles— in other words, with their own bottoms up. Ambassador Cru came erect like a mechanized toy, which in some ways he resembled, his clothes, his mustachios—with eyebrows matching them, sheenly black—impeccable, a jewelled sash across his breast. Another poor boy who had made good, the General thought wryly, taking a hand weighted with a diamond ring. Cru represented a Latin American country which still bore strong traces of French influence, and Cru himself was a curious mixture. The General thought him pompous, antiquated and interesting only as money interested one. Which it did this one. The other gentleman wore more sheen on the highly polished bottom of his dress suit than anywhere else. The General recognized him, however, Joshua Katz, the violinist, and introduced himself.

"You're playing here next Thursday, aren't you?"

Katz shot his cuffs out from his coat sleeves. "I am."

"Sold out, I understand," the General said. "We're not all philistines, by God. It makes a man perk up to hear that when he's just about had it up to the apple."

"So I have," Katz said, assuming ridiculously that the General was being solicitous of him.

"In my country," the Latin American said ponderously, "we are partial to the piano."

It was on the tip of the General's tongue to say that in his country they were also partial to the nut, but he forebore. He poured himself a glass of sherry, a tribute to the wines his host would serve at dinner.

"I'll have a man's drink," Katz said, and hooked into the Scotch.

"I hope it suffices," the General said, and moved on toward the great parlour as the violinist turned and glowered after him. He surveyed the rest of the guests from the doorway.

His host came up and pressed his elbow in gentle persuasion. "You're going to be well taken care of at dinner, Ransom."

"I trust by women," the General said, looking up from under his brows. It was his habit to lower his head when he felt bullish. And obviously, when he felt it, he looked it.

His host nodded gravely. "A virtual harem to attend you."

If it was to be drawn from those present, the General thought, he might as well be a eunuch.

Senator Grace Chisholm was here. She stood head and shoulders above most men in the Senate, a frightening thought. Also present was an ageing opera singer, Maria Candido. He had heard once that she had the most extensive repertoire of bawdy songs in America. But to have to deliver them in a coloratura soprano the General thought downright indecent. The ambassador's wife flapped her eyelashes at him like Venetian blinds every time he glanced her way. He was reasonably certain nothing was going on behind them, and even more certain that he was not going to find out. And then there was Madam Secretary Elizabeth Jennings of the presidential cabinet. She was the only woman present the General had not spoken to, but she seemed at the moment to have caught for herself the only animate creature in the room, a very slim young man who seemed, from the distance at which the General explored him, a trifle seedy; "quaint" might be the word, for he wore his hair long, in a style known some years before as a pompadour, and the collar of his dress shirt was high.

The General elbowed his host. "Who's the young chap?"

"Talking to Madam Jennings?" the General nodded. "Young man about town," Chatterton said off-handedly. "His name is Montaigne—or something like that."

Chatterton was trying to be matter-of-fact, trying too hard, the General thought, and his curiosity was but the more whetted. He leaned toward his host. "Does he belong to anyone I know?"

Chatterton was not amused. "He's what you might call social provender, Ransom. An acquaintance of Laura's, and several others of tonight's guests."

No declared occupation, the General thought, and in a town where every man needed a title as much as he needed the job it came with. He did not, however, pursue the subject with his host. He could tell by the squint of Chatterton's eye and a shadowy nervous twitching at its corner that something was aggravating an old disorder. "A bit off tonight, Ed? The old ulcer?"

Chatterton laughed, but without mirth. "To tell the God's truth, Ransom, I can't tell the old one from the new one these days."

"Bad, bad," the General murmured solicitously.

"No foundation all the way down the line," Chatterton said in something like a confidential whisper.

The General could not remember what he was quoting, but he understood from its present context. There was no one in Chatterton's branch of service with genuine authority who would stand firm, and everybody was swinging at the State Department, especially Senator Fagan.

"There's a man, Fagan," the General said, "who goes looking for the cracked bricks under a house. Pulls them out for all he's worth. I hope he finds out that most of us have a little crack in us somewhere, and still manage to hold up our end. I hope he finds it out before he pulls the whole place down on top of us."

Chatterton stood with the polite air of a man waiting for him to be done. Then he said, "I rang you up at the club today. Understand you're living at home now."

"It's where they've got to take you in whether or not you've got the cash," the General said. "Introduce me to Madam Jennings, will you, Ed?"

"Good God, forgive me. I hadn't known you were not acquainted."

"We met once, but it's a long time ago and I don't want to risk her not remembering."

In truth, what the General wanted was to observe his host

and the young fop together, to measure the depth of their
familiarity if he could. He did not think of himself as a snob,
but on the whole he thought this a bottom-drawer assortment of people to gather in this house. Secretary Jennings was
the exception, and he supposed Senator Chisholm, although
she was a bit wholesome for his tastes; and by God, he was an
exception himself!

He was not to have the chance now to observe Montaigne
and his host. The young man, seeing them approach, managed to
wind up his talk with Secretary Jennings and spin off at precisely
the instant before introductions would have been necessary.

Chatterton said, "Madam Secretary, may I present an old
friend, Ransom Jarvis, major general, United States Army?"

"I believe we've met, General Jarvis." She gave his hand a
firm grasp. There was foundation there all the way down the
line.

"You were a little girl in Newport when we first met. I was
a West Point plebe, I think."

"I didn't know my memory was that long," she said, and
there was something rather sad in the way she said it that
set the General to speculating on what he might have interrupted. His memory of her dated more recently than he had
said: to some wartime mission in London when he had met
her briefly—and in the company of many military men of
several countries—and had thought her then a woman of
enormous attractiveness. Ah, but circumstances were different
now, and so was Elizabeth Jennings. She had grown plump
and plain as a suet pudding.

"I hope I didn't frighten the young man off," the General said, looking round as though he expected him to be standing nearby.

"I doubt it," Madam Jennings said.

"I seem to have that way about me lately—people run from me as from an old bull terrier for all that he may be nodding and toothless."

"Do you know him?" The woman's gaze was trailing after Montaigne as he crossed the room. She had not heard a word the General had said about himself.

"Certainly not."

Madam Secretary lifted her head, a show of pride perhaps, and looked him straight in the eye. She was a woman of considerable social poise and long political experience, but, the General thought she could not hide her regret at his having interrupted the attentions of the younger man, and she refused to be ashamed of it. It made him feel sad himself, lugubrious, in fact.

"I wonder if we both couldn't do with a drink? May I bring you something, Madam Secretary?"

"You're very kind. I would like a sherry." She smiled on him with the sudden joy of one reprieved.

His humour was restored, along with his confidence in himself as a judge of women. He found his best prospect of the evening so far to be the company of his own thoughts, a vigilant contemplation of the relationship between a young sport and a fifty-year-old spinster.

On the way to the bar he purposely brushed against the

man. It forced them to introduce themselves. Looking into his eyes, the expression in which seemed deliberately covert, like a lascivious cleric's, and further judging him by the deliberate droop of his shape, the languid pose, the General would now call him a young decadent. He hadn't seen anything quite like him since European society just before World War I, and perhaps the American imitation of it after that war. He gave his name as Leo Montaigne. The General wondered out of what novel he had taken it.

"Sorry to have cut in on your conversation with Secretary Jennings," the General said. "Didn't mean to, you know. Just wanted to meet the lady."

"And understandable that you should." Montaigne raised his voice a little. The woman in question was approaching. "All men seem to, and she is lovable, don't you agree, sir?"

"Adorable," the General replied, and it could have been as handily said of a Sherman tank. The insolent pup, to have so involved him. He bulled his neck and charged on toward the bar.

Chatterton once more intercepted him. "Oh, come, Ransom, surely it's not that bad?"

"If rotten is bad, it's that bad," the General said. "Where the hell did you get him? I'm surprised at Laura. And I'll tell her so, myself."

Chatterton straightened himself up, and it seemed to give him pain to do it. "Is it any of your business, Ransom?"

"No, I suppose it's not." He got hold of himself. "I'm being ridiculous, eh?"

"Let me say this, he has many friends for whom he does many favours."

This time the General truly did not understand and said so.

"Neither do I, Ransom, but I have a feeling he would make a deadly enemy."

In that the General concurred. "All right, old man. I promise—no fuss."

Chatterton was again completely affable. "Here's Dr. d'Inde, one of the great art curators. You know him, don't you?"

The General stared for an instant at the tall, good looking man then bending low over the hand of his hostess. "No. Don't know him."

"Come along and I'll introduce you, a splendid fellow. He'll be more to your liking. I understand he's fathered seven children."

"I'd rather meet the mother," the General growled.

He started to follow his host, but at that moment another feminine guest was announced, and this one, by the heavens, was really feminine. Every man in the room added an inch to his stature the instant she came into view. The General forgot the introduction to d'Inde, the drink he had promised Madam Secretary and himself; he even forgot his ill humour and considered it a good omen that he was mobile and able, thus, to arrive at the side of the latest guest before any other man could disengage himself.

"How do you do?" the General said.

"Oh, I know *you*," she said in a voice that had a pleasant sort of rattle to it. Flat and somewhat nasal, it had nonetheless a warm, gay quality.

34

"That, then, is but one of the many advantages you have over me," he said, and bent low over her spangled fingertips.

She gave his hand a little squeeze in delightful contrast to the pumpings he'd been having by the hands of women lately. "I'm Virginia Allan," she said. "It's an assumed name, of course. I mean I assumed it myself—honourably." Her smile was sudden, and the twinkle went on in her blue eyes at the same time.

"I'm sure nothing you do could be less than honourable for your doing it, Miss Allan." He cleared his throat. Something there was a bit thick.

"General Jarvis, you dear!"

With that, she flitted away from him. She was blonde—something else assumed honourably he thought, looking after her. Her walk reminded him of a mermaid, not altogether ridiculously, for her dress was sequined and snug to the toes. She was neatly put together entirely he thought, and long enough ago that he need not coddle his conscience should the opportunity for other coddling present itself. Realizing that his eyes were trailing across the room after her, he pulled himself up and glanced about in time to catch a look of austere disapproval from—of all people—the young pup, Leo. The disconcerting thought then occurred to him: she might just possibly be Leo's mother.

At that moment the Latin American ambassador came out of the study, and across the room he and Montaigne discovered one another, and with loud acclaims broke up everybody else's conversation. They met and embraced, and immediately fell to reminiscences about Paris, the Riviera and Capri. There was something mesmeric about it all the same, something of an old enchantment that drew almost everyone in the room to them. Even Katz the musician, lounging at the study door, was caught up in it, his pouched eyes dreamy, his mouth as slack as it was sometimes said his musicianship had gone of late. " . . . And the night," Montaigne was saying, "I couldn't find a stitch to put on when somebody turned in the fire alarm . . . You see the dilemma, of course . . ." (This remark was an aside to Mrs. Chatterton. The General got the feeling that some people there had heard it before and were encouraging its retelling.) " . . . The question was whether to go down *on* or *in* the bed sheets."

"And what did you do?"

"Well, as a matter of fact, I took a pillowcase, and tore two holes in the seam for my legs, ran the service bellcord through the hem at my waist, and went down on the sheets in that. The costume had a certain charm—with me in it. It became quite a fashion that season. You couldn't buy a pillowcase in all Nice."

"Ah, Nice," said the opera singer. "I know a lovely ballad— in French (this to the host), so don't be alarmed. If Joshua would bring me a drink I might sing it." She cast her eyes on the violinist. "Dear Josh."

If he had a drink himself, the General thought, he might listen. Going in quest of it, however, he found Miss Allan.

"I'll just bet you've had some wonderful experiences your-self, General."

"A few more, I dare say, than that young man," he said, with as much modesty as he could manage.

"Are you what they call a field general?"

"I beg pardon?"

"What I mean is, were you in real danger—I mean from the enemy?"

"And occasionally from my friends," the General said. "Will you have a drink with me, Miss Allan?"

"I'd love to, General. I've never known a real military man of rank. My last army friend turned out to be a corporal when he put his uniform on."

"They're the most dangerous of all."

"Corporals, you mean?"

The General nodded. "Napoleon and Hitler."

"I never think of them as corporals."

"Most people don't," the General said, "but I've got a feeling they never got over thinking of it themselves."

Virginia giggled. "I know somebody just like that—going round acting like a general. I don't mean you, honey, you don't act like a general at all."

"Perhaps because I was never a corporal," he said. "What will you drink, my dear?"

A few minutes later dinner was announced.

6

General Jarvis sat at his hostess' left, the ambassador at her right. To the ambassador's right sat Senator Chisholm. It occurred to the General she was a ranking member of the Armed Services Committee. In his own best interests, a man in his position should curry favour with the old girl this night; he would never have a better opportunity. But on the General's left was Virginia Allan, and he was unlikely to have a better opportunity to curry her favour either.

It was remarkable the career so attractive a woman could have behind her, a try at so many occupations; a new one showed up at every turn in the conversation. There was something almost kittenish about her—not in the disgusting, coy manner, but in the sudden ingratiating twists she gave things, dipping daintily into one provocative bit of talk after another. The General was hard put to give their hostess any part of his attention.

But she needed it, he realized, sending her a sidelong glance. She was working as hard tonight as Ed was, and she ordinarily throve on such doings. Her whole mind turned to it, like a morning glory stretching for sun. Now he could see her stretch her lips to make a smile. He complimented her on the dinner, and then ran dry. The best he could do was include her addressing himself to the ambassador.

"When were you on the Riviera last, Excellency?"

"Such a long time ago," Cru said. "Was it 1928? Laura, do you remember?"

Mrs. Chatterton said hastily, "It must have been." Hastily, to avoid particulars? the General wondered. "I saw a ring around the moon last night. I hope it won't rain tonight. It would ruin the ball." She rattled on. "Do you remember the play, *Dark of the Moon*?"

"Are you having superstitions, Laura?" the ambassador asked.

"Oh, no."

But she was having something, the General thought, something she was unlikely to confide in him. Thank God. He turned back to Virginia Allan as soon as he could. "Curious," he said, "there are some women with whom it is absolutely impossible for me to strike up a conversation."

"You are kind of forbidding, General."

"I have never forbidden a woman anything in my life, to

my sorrow," he said. "And couldn't you manage to call me 'Ransom', Miss Allan . . . Virginia, if I may?"

"I think Ransom is just a lovely name . . . Ransom. It's so—southern."

"Old family attachment," he murmured.

"Really?" she said brightly. "Were they pirates?"

The General cleared his throat. So charmingly naïve. "Horse thieves," he said. "That's how I came to start in the cavalry."

"Ransom, you're pulling my leg," she said.

The General thought the better of what he was about to say, and merely sounded a rumble deep in his throat.

"What you were saying about women and conversation," Virginia said, laying down her fish fork, "you know, Ransom, some women can't talk to anybody unless they're telling secrets."

"But I love secrets," the General protested.

"You love women, too, don't you?"

"Especially women with secrets."

Virginia laughed. She might even be blushing, he thought, but that was hard to tell. It was not very long thereafter—during the fowl course, after the first sip of a fine Rhone wine—that he proposed they go on to the ball together. "Unless you'd prefer not to go to the ball?"

"Oh," she said, "what a naughty idea!"

"My dear, I am a patron of the arts, but that does not compel me to fraternize with the artists. That boor next to you—once a pretty good violinist . . ."

"Monsieur Katz?"

"What did you say?"

She repeated, a lovely light whisper to her French.

He leaned close to her ear and said, "I thought you were calling me 'pussy cat'."

She found the impulse to laugh irresistible, and he found her laughter contagious so that he joined it, although to be sure, behind his napkin. An embarrassed silence hung round the table in the wake of their mirth.

"You had better take care, General," the ambassador volunteered his advice. "There are times it is not good to laugh."

"Oh, now, go on, Your Excellency," Miss Allan joshed. "Laughter's good for anybody any time."

"There are times," Cru said, again ponderous, "when a man can die of it."

The General had got coldly sober. "I think I shall escape that fate for the present," he said, "or at least in the present company." He looked down the table from under his brows. "I beg your pardons." For a few moments he gave the bird on his plate his complete attention. Virginia was talking softly to M. Katz and Laura and the ambassador were apparently recalling a number of asphyxiations among their acquaintanceship.

There was something very strange about this party, and now and then he got the feeling of almost understanding it, of its breaking through to him. He thought about his hostess: Virginia's remark about women who could really talk only in secrets had validity. Laura might very well be one of them;

what she was now saying to Cru seemed in the nature of a confidence. Confidences was a better word than secrets. He fell to musing on where she might have met Ed . . . and Cru, whom she seemed to have known in France. There! He almost had that elusive thing about the party, the peculiarity.

But at that instant Senator Chisholm said, "Cheese." She represented a dairy state.

The General put down his silver with a clatter. Few things offended him more than talk of one food while he was eating another. There was also some sort of fuss in the making at the other end of the table. The art man, d'Inde, had blown up a temper.

Across the table from him was Montaigne, sitting next to Secretary Jennings, a social elevation the General was at a loss to understand.

"I meant nothing personal, I assure you, doctor," Montaigne said. The General was pleased to see him, too, hoisted now on the silence. "I was merely thinking how necessary geographic expansion becomes with the steady increase of population. Mind you, I'm all for increasing population. I should even approve some sort of bounty on every child."

"Now you sound like Mussolini," d'Inde said.

"I admire him," Montaigne said blandly.

A murmur of surprise came from some at the table.

"More to the point of practicality," the General interposed, "why not admire Hitler? Someday you may be able to bring him up alive."

Young Montaigne glowered at him, his soft good looks

shrouded in fury. "I deny that those two men are comparable—in any way whatever."

The General shook his head, amused to have provoked such contention on an issue he considered not merely academic, but dead. He wondered if Montaigne were serious or simply without humour.

"Virginia," he said, turning to her when a murmur of conversation resumed, "do you know that young man?"

"Leo?" she said. "Of course I do. He's my boyfriend."

It was remarkable, the General thought, sitting back and taking a long drink of his wine, how quickly a duck could turn out to be a drake.

"Only I'll tell you the honest truth, Ransom, he's a little young for me," she added after a moment.

"He's a little young for me, too," the General said dryly. But he tightened the muscles in his arms and relaxed them just to be sure they were working. He could think of several blisters he would have liked to deliver at the moment to his host and hostess for such arrangements. If they had drawn their guests by lot they could not have been more ill assorted.

"Where were you thinking of us going, Ransom? I mean, instead of going to the ball?"

"I had no place special in mind," he said, "and I suppose we should put in an appearance there."

"Why?"

"Protocol, you might say."

"Oh," she said. "I thought maybe it was on account of Leo."

"Certainly not."

"'Cause he won't be there."

"Oh?"

"Don't you know the *Club Sentimentale*?"

"No."

"That's Leo's place. I sing for him sometimes."

"I thought you told me you were a nurse these days," the General said.

"Honey, I do that in my spare time." She smiled at him dazzlingly. "Singing, I mean, naturally. I don't have a very good voice really, but it's full of nostalgia. You know what I mean?" Beneath the elegant damask tablecloth her dainty little hand found his and lingered but a persuasive second.

"Unequivocally," he said.

"I'm my own mistress, Ransom," she went on, "and I'll tell you the honest truth: I'd love to spend an evening in the company of an older man."

The "honest truth" again gave him pause. The truth was one thing, but to have to be honest about it—it was like a naked nude, just too much of a good thing.

"Do you have an automobile, Ransom?"

"I drive a Jaguar," he said loftily.

"Oh, Ransom, do you? I think they're absolutely sexy."

7

Jimmie and Helene arrived at the ball early, hoping in that way to depart early, inconspicuously. It was the first Washington function at which he had not been among the available younger men, and he was very popular among the hostesses—his politics, his family, his fortune being irresistible recommendations. Consequently, his fashionable acquaintance gave Helene a severe scrutiny.

"I can take it," she said. "After all, I started public life as a model."

Jimmie frowned a little.

Helene laughed. "If I didn't know the heart under that stuffed shirt, Jimmie, I'd be devastated."

"It's not stuffed. It's stiff, that's all. My stiff upper shirt."

"Something every congressman must have, no doubt," Helene said.

"Absolutely."

"Would you like me to tell you why?"

"All right," he said. "You tell me why."

"It's something you can't wash in public."

Jimmie looked at her in pained dismay. "Don't you think we had better dance?"

It was a lovely, long, spiralling waltz into which he took her in full sail. The floor was all but given over to them for the stately command of their dancing. There was something about a waltz, Jimmie remarked at its end, that made chaperons expendable: if a couple danced it well, they need pass no other test of propriety. All the elegant old girls nodded approvingly upon the congressman and his friend; she was now quite acceptable.

"I wonder where Father is," Jimmie said. The music had stopped as they neared the great doors, and Jimmie saw Secretary Chatterton and Mrs. Senator Grace Chisholm and Henri d'Inde. Jimmie would have liked to divert Helene from the Frenchman's line of vision. Too late. He came with as much haste as he could, having to steer the senator with him.

D'Inde made all the introductions.

"You look like a midwesterner, girl," the senator said.

Helene smiled. "My ancestors came from there."

"Now isn't that a switch?" Grace Chisholm said. "Mine came from New England. What about yours, Congressman?"

"New York State," Jimmie said. D'Inde was asking Helene to dance, of course.

"Which side of the Hudson?"

"The American side," Jimmie said, which was rather tart for him; more like his father. Unlike his father, he attempted to atone immediately. "May I have the next dance, Senator?" He had never heard anything that sounded more ridiculous, a man saying May I have the next dance, Senator? More to the point: choose your weapons, sir!

"Bless you, Jarvis, I haven't danced since corn-shucking time of '45. The Japanese had just surrendered and I knew my boys were coming home safe." For an instant the eyes, normally clear and wide as a prairie sky, clouded. Then the senator frowned. She nodded toward the door and said, "And between you and me, sir, I think the next time I dance is going to be at the political demise of the junior senator from a neighbouring state of mine."

Jimmie followed the direction of her gaze. Senator Fagan had just arrived. "I hope I'll be here to dance with you, Senator," he said, and walked her toward the palms. "You haven't by any chance seen my father since dinner?"

"Your father?" The senator stopped and looked at him.

"General Ransom Jarvis," Jimmie said, not without inner qualms at the look he was getting from her.

"No, sir, not since dinner," she said curtly. "I can go on from here myself, Congressman. Thank you."

Oh, Lord, Jimmie thought, what has he done now? He stood at the edge of the ballroom floor, his hands behind his back, and looked over the dancers. His father had always been a great one for dancing. Oh, damn his father! He was not his keeper. Still, he would like to know who else had attended the Chatterton dinner party. He gradually became aware that a few paces off, Senator Fagan was doing the same thing he was, standing, his hands in his pockets, surveying the dancers. Jimmie wondered if it was his imagination that suggested a tension in the room, an automatous quality coming over the dance. What was the power of this man? What lay behind the dark, sneering eyes, the contemptuous grin of one who seemed himself to enjoy trouble and therefore felt it his duty to create it for others? His following was considerable and, no less than most men's following, with honest people among it: his man, Tom Hennessy, thought Fagan was great.

Of one thing Jimmie was sure: the spontaneity had gone out of the ball with Fagan's arrival. And still he stood, rocking back and forth, as though waiting. Jimmie could feel his own nerves go taut. Why? Why could one man's watching do this—and to honest men? Or were not perhaps the honest even more vulnerable? Were they not the innocent bystanders who lost their innocence standing by? Oh, damn Fagan, too! He wasn't his keeper either!

But Fagan then did something that really set his nerves on edge: as Helene and d'Inde passed close to him, dancing toward Jimmie, the senator turned his head and watched them right to the point where they left the dance floor to join Jimmie. He continued to stare while d'Inde took a handkerchief from his pocket, wiped his hands, his brow and his upper lip. Their dancing had not been that strenuous. Fagan grinned, shrugged, and turned elsewhere.

"What's the matter with d'Inde?" Jimmie said when he and Helene were alone.

"I don't know. Terribly tense, and he wasn't this afternoon."

"Why isn't he home with his wife and seven children?"

Helene countered quite tellingly: "I understand your father was smitten tonight."

"With what?" said Jimmie, as though he didn't know.

"Something blonde and . . . oh, you know."

If he didn't know, he should have, Jimmie thought. "Do you know her name?"

"Virginia Allan."

"Does she sing ballads?" he said hopefully.

"Blues," Helene said throatily. "I understand she sings in a club."

"What the devil is Chatterton doing, having someone like that to dinner?" Jimmie exploded. Helene shook her head. "I suppose I knew from the night he came to tell me they were retiring him," Jimmie said. "I knew something like this would happen."

"I think it's charming," Helene said. "I've never known a man to maintain so romantic a household as you do. Your secretary is quite handsome, by the way. I meant to tell you."

"When did you meet her?"

"Him," Helene corrected.

Jimmie thought for a moment. "Hennessy?"

"He brought me your flowers this afternoon, dear."

"The Irish rogue! I told him to have them sent. And he's not my secretary. I doubt if he can sign his own name."

"I shouldn't be surprised if he can sign yours though," Helene said. "He has the same sort of devilry about him that your father has, and an eye for art—though perhaps not for its own sake. Henri spoke to him rather severely."

"Henri was there for art's sake, of course," Jimmie said.

"Darling, is that Senator Fagan?"

"Yes."

"He has fascinating eyes, hasn't he?"

Jimmie came very close to saying something vulgar. Instead, he danced. Almost everyone did, at least one dance, in the course of the evening. But not Senator Fagan. He merely stood on the side and watched, a twitch of a grin now and then on his face. Senator Chisholm remarked he was like a carnival shill. Occasionally he would jerk his head in greeting to someone he recognized; but very few people felt more comfortable for the protective gaze he cast upon them.

It was almost midnight when the commotion started. Jimmie and Helene heard first that someone had fainted, then that it was Under Secretary of State Chatterton's wife, then that it had happened when someone showed her a copy of a morning newspaper; the rumours flowed out from the vicinity of the unfortunate woman like circles in a pond from a flung stone.

Jimmie finally got hold of a copy of the newspaper. It was the early edition of the Washington *Journal*, and in it, headlined, was Senator Fagan's latest exposé: at one of the gold-plate dinners preceding the Beaux Arts Ball, a dinner hosted by a prominent member of the State Department, at least four of the twelve people present were known security risks or subversives.

Jimmie sought out Senator Chisholm. "Who are the four? Do you know whom he means?"

"You're looking at one right now," the senator said, "for all I know. He's the first farmer I ever knew didn't look which way the wind was blowing before he pitched manure."

The senator was kind enough then to recall for him the names of the Chatterton's guests.

"Most of them aren't even in government service," Jimmie said. "By heavens, I'm going to confront him right now, and see what he has to say about Father."

"You'd better hurry, Congressman, if you think you can catch up with his carrion."

For just an instant, Jimmie was prompted by her bitterness to wonder how vulnerable Senator Chisholm really was. Then he cursed himself for having caught the infection. But that was what it was like throughout the great domed ballroom, throughout the capital city itself, old friends sudden unsuspecting suspects, each to the other, and no one so touched, however fleetingly, ever quite innocent again.

Jimmie looked everywhere for Senator Fagan, going finally to the men's cloakroom. The senator had left the ball a few moments earlier.

8

Not long after leaving the Chatterton dinner the General and Miss Virginia Allan sped out of the city and into the Virginia hills. The air was clear and crisp, the moon full. Virginia was bundled in furs, not quite expensive, but not quite cheap either. The General, as was his custom driving, wore a great wool scarf around his neck. They were in the country, he mused, where the Civil War might have been earlier won with boldness, or early lost by rashness. Lincoln's commander then was neither bold nor rash, merely ambitious. At times, General Jarvis realized, he was himself in danger of being rash, and he was now weighing certain intimations of possible disaster. Like any military man, he did not trust the promise of easy conquest.

"Ransom, you drive like a cavalier, I do declare."

The farther south they got, the more southern did Miss Allan become, he noticed. But why not? After all, this was her country. It was her cabin in the hills toward which they were heading. Just how she happened to have a cabin in the hills, he did not care to contemplate. Maybe she had a pappy there with a shotgun. A fine scandal in the making there! But he thought not. Whoever, whatever she was, she was not the "pappy" type.

He laid his hand on hers where it snuggled in her lap. "Thank you, my dear, for the compliment."

"What's that little knob for, Ransom?" She disengaged her hand gently and pointed to the dashboard.

He explained. In fact, in twenty miles he had spent ten of them explaining the operational ways of the Jaguar. But some women were like that. It wasn't that they wanted the information at all, but that they thought it flattered a man to ask it of him. Or else they wanted to keep him talking. He doubted that to be Virginia's purpose.

"It's the next right turn, Ransom."

He slowed the Jaguar down to a growl, and turned onto a small wooden bridge.

"Oh, Ransom, I'm sorry, honey," she cried. "This isn't it. I make this mistake all the time. It's a little way yonder, our turn."

"Which way is yonder?" He threw the car into reverse.

"Like we were going. There, see that road?"

It occurred to the General that this might have been as

good a way as any to signal ahead to someone looking out for their coming. His service revolver was under the driver's seat, but where the devil was he to carry it on his person, wearing tails? It was one way for a man to shoot his brains out, presuming them to be where the General had begun to think his were this night.

"I got the most beautiful view, Ransom."

He looked down at her, wondering if she was reading his mind at that instant.

"From my cabin. You'll love it in the moonlight."

"That's what I'm looking forward to, Virginia, that beautiful view in the moonlight."

"I want to hear just everything about your career, Ransom. We haven't begun to discover one another, have we?"

"Certainly not."

"You said you were in the war, didn't you?"

"Mmmm."

"Did you have some—experiences?"

"Mmmmm."

"With—foreigners?"

The General spared her a quick glance. "About which war are you inquiring, my dear?"

The Jaguar seemed to be shinnying up a washboard. It banished conversation. Then they reached a plateau, the road levelling off and disappearing. Before them an unlit cabin huddled in the moonlight, seeming to start up like something alive when the car's lights flashed onto the glass of the windows.

"There!" Virginia said. "This is my little house."

It looked folksy enough to have hovelled a president, the General thought.

The Jaguar nosed up to it like a hound dog. "Steady, boy," the General murmured.

Virginia waited for him to get out and come around the car to open the door for her. The demand on his gallantry settled the matter of whether or not to take his service revolver with him. It was an altogether foolish notion anyway, he thought, once out in the still night beauty. The fresh green smell of spring was in the air, and then he caught a scent that took him quite a long way back in memory, to summers he had once spent on a farm: it was the acrid smell of silage—chopped, fermented corn. Unless, by God, "pappy" ran a still!

Virginia gave him the key to the cabin door. As soon as he opened it, a dark, smoky fireplace odour pervaded.

"I reckon I should have my chimney cleaned," she said. "But every spring there's a family of thrushes settle in there, and I can't bear to trouble them."

The electric lamps, as she went from one to another, illuminated a room which looked much cosier than it felt, and it had not been decorated with the airy flounces he expected of Virginia Allan. In fact, he would take his oath it had been done with the strong, square taste of a long-legged man. What the hell had he expected? Decidedly he was beginning to feel a little shoddy about the whole enterprise.

"Shall I make a fire?" the General suggested more cheerfully than his spirits warranted.

"Not in the fireplace!"

"Where, then, would you suggest, my dear?"

"It's going to be comfy any minute now, Ransom, I just turned the heat on."

You did that a couple of hours ago, he thought, but he said, "Electricity?"

Virginia nodded. "Terribly extravagant of me, isn't it?"

"Depends," the General said. "Depends entirely." And there he let the matter stand.

"You just go in the kitchen, Ransom, and fix us a nice drink while I get into something comfy."

He wished to God he could get into something comfy. It sure as hell wouldn't be a log cabin. But he bumbled his way into the kitchen, and discovered a fine assortment of whiskies and brandies. He could feel the radiant heat edging out from the corners, and he began to get a better perspective on things. Considerably to his pleasure, when Virginia reappeared she was wearing—not the obvious, well, not the obvious obvi-ous—but a skirt and cashmere sweater.

"Exquisite," he murmured, and gently brushed up the nap with the back of his fingers.

"I just knew you were that kind of a man," Virginia said purringly.

Most men were, the General supposed. It was characteris-tic of the species. He said, "Brandy or whisky?"

"A touch of Scotch, please."

The General was reminded of Mrs. Norris. He frowned.

"There," Virginia said, "you just thought of an old love, didn't you?"

"Well, somebody's old love. I was just thinking of ... a house-keeper." He hesitated, Mrs. Norris being Jimmie's housekeeper, and his having no intention at that moment of dragging in the subject of a middle-aged son.

Virginia smiled at him brightly. "Would you like a house-keeper, Ransom?"

"Depends," he said. "Depends entirely."

Virginia laughed and clicked her glass to his. "I do believe you're shy. I don't want you to be, honey. I've been looking forward ever since dinnertime to a nice evening of conversa-tion. I just love conversation. Especially with an intelligent man."

The General took a long, deep draught of whisky and soda. "Don't you think you're going on an unwarranted assump-tion?"

"Beg pardon?"

"What makes you take for granted I'm intelligent?"

"Well, you're rich, aren't you?"

That, of course, was the most unwarranted assumption of all, but the General didn't say so. He was oddly assured by the directness, the honesty of her answer. She was, after all, just a sim-ple girl. He padded happily after her back into the living room.

"Ransom, I got a sloppy Joe sweater I swear would fit you. Wouldn't you like to get out of that starched shirt for just a little while?" He allowed her to bring the sweater, a black and white striped affair, the stripes fortunately vertical. She opened it out. "I do believe there's enough room for both of us in it."

The General blinked his eyes mischievously. "Shall we try it on?"

Virginia put it in his hands and thrust him on his way with the same motion. "You go right back in the kitchen there and put it on you."

The General did as he was bade. Having thrust his head through the turtle neck, he caught a glimpse of himself reflected in the kitchen window, his hair on end, his complexion ruddy, his chest capacious. "Coach," he said at the image derisively. All he needed now was a pair of goddamned skis.

9

Tom Hennessy, as was his custom, had gone out for the paper just before bedtime. He pushed the cat off the chair and sat down at the kitchen table, where he read aloud to Mrs. Norris the story of Senator Fagan's latest sensation. He was enjoying himself in a way she thought would have better become a football match than the investigations of the United States Senate.

"Does he give the names of the people?" she asked.

"There'll be names in the later editions, never mind," said Hennessy. "He has to clean out the stables before he can count the horses."

Mrs. Norris sighed. "I don't altogether approve him," she felt compelled to say. "He makes some very wild allegations."

"Of course he does! Would you expect tame ones with what's going on in the country?"

Mrs. Norris tried to hold to her own line of reasoning. "And I don't approve of people informing on one another. Let me finish, Tom Hennessy: it was one of the things I always admired in the Irish up till now, the way they had no use among one another for informers."

"There's informers and informers!" Hennessy cried, and whacked his fist on the table. "It all depends on who's informing on who."

Mrs. Norris opened her mouth and then closed it again without saying anything. The front doorbell was ringing, and the hour past midnight. Tom sat where he was, his fist doubled on the table.

"Can you not move, man?" Mrs. Norris cried.

"You want me to open it?"

"Aren't you the butler?"

"Oh, aye," Tom said. "I keep forgetting." He put on the black silk coat Mrs. Norris was holding for him. It apparently had come with the house, but it took her to find a use for it.

"There. You look sartorial," she said, which was not quite the right word, but close, and she wanted to flatter him into the role.

"Do I now?" he said cockily, and went through the house at a glide over the polished floors. He opened the door to an erect, elegant gentleman in full dress and sparkling sash. Tom thought he had never seen anything as startling as his stiff black mustachios with the matching eyebrows.

"Who are you?" said the stranger.

"Wasn't it you rang the bell?" Tom said warily. He could see the chauffeured car in the moonlight, a bruiser of a fellow standing beside it.

The gentleman clicked his heels. "I am Ambassador Cru," he said, and named the country he represented. "This is the Jarvis residence? Am I wrong?"

"You are right and I am the Jarvis . . ."Tom could not bring himself to say the word butler. Instead his tongue leaped to all the things he wanted and expected soon to be. "I am the boss' secretary, his confidential man, his friend and his faithful servant." After which recitation, he almost kicked one heel out from under himself with the other, and for good measure, saluted smartly.

"You are in position then to act as second for him, yes?"

It occurred to Tom that he was about to be asked to stand in for the boss at some diplomatic function he had no time for. And sure it was the boss' place to tell him whether or not he could, not this fellow's.

"Yes!" he said with less hesitation than so much thought would seem to require.

"Good!" The ambassador flashed a white card into Tom's hand. "M. Montaigne's card, sir. He calls your master out for having insulted him in the matter of the lady on whom he forced his attentions this evening. He is therefore challenged to duel to the death for honour's sake at dawn. We shall expect you at the river's edge on the Arlington side of the Key Bridge. Are you agreed?"

"With what?" Tom sputtered.

"Naturally you may choose the weapons. May I suggest pistols?"

"Pistols?" said Tom.

"Excellent. M. Montaigne will provide them." The ambassador rubbed his hands in grim satisfaction. "At your service, sir. As a gentleman to a gentleman, I salute you."

As a gentleman to a gentleman, Tom was not sure that he should not let him have a left to the jaw. But the dapper little diplomat clicked his heels, whirled and ran down the steps. The chauffeur flung open the door of the black limousine, folded his arms across his chest like the crossbones of a skeleton while the ambassador entered the car. He closed the door and leaped into the front seat. In seconds the limousine disappeared, slithering into the night like a well-groomed panther.

Tom banged the front door and all but skated back to the kitchen. "Lord, lord, wait till you hear this, Mrs. Norris! Will you get something and write this down before it goes out of my mind?"

Tom clapped his head as though to hold in the thought while Mrs. Norris got a pencil from beside the phone and brought it to the porcelain-topped table. "Let me hear it," she said.

"The boss is to be under the Key Bridge . . ."

"What bridge?" she interrupted.

"Key—like in the Star Spangled Banner."

Mrs. Norris wrote the words. "Go on."

"On the Arlington side at dawn." Tom drew a great breath and sighed with relief.

Mrs. Norris wrote "Arlington side" and then stopped. "Mr. James will not get up that early."

"He'll have to tomorrow. He's challenged to a duel."

"Nonsense. Someone played you a joke. The Irish are very gullible."

"Gullible, is it? Then look at this." He held the card in front of her nose. "This one's to be there with pistols and the ambassador of some South American country, and I'm to be there and bring the boss."

Mrs. Norris held the card to the light. "Leo Montaigne," she read, pronouncing each syllable carefully.

Tom squinted at it over her shoulder. "Couldn't that name be said 'Mon-tan'?"

"I suppose it could. I've heard of 'Mon-tan'."

"Then I've got it all," said Tom, "and I can tell you, it's no joke. Remember me telling you this afternoon about the Frenchman I met at the boss' girlfriend's? Didn't I say his name rhymed with 'Dan', well?"

"All right, you said it," Mrs. Norris said.

"Now listen to what this fella said at the door: 'monseur'—that fellow's—card sir. He challenges your master to duel at dawn for having insulted him over the lady he forced his attentions on tonight.' Or words to that effect. And he said we could have our choice of the pistols this fella would bring."

Mrs. Norris folded the newspaper and fanned herself vigorously. "It sounds more like the General than Mr. James' affairs," she said.

"Will you stop confusing matters?" Tom roared. "You're as contrary as a cow's hind leg. You just arrived here today. You don't understand what tempers are like in this town. And you should've heard the boss when he was getting dressed tonight, about the French artist fella meeting her at the airport this morning in striped trousers and frock coat . . ."

Mrs. Norris sat down and buried her chin in her fist. She was hearing now for the first time the reason Mr. James had not met her himself this morning: he had been at the airport meeting Mrs. Joyce. And she knew, as truth was truth, it must have been a hard choice for him to make, and perhaps after all, the Frenchman had something to do with it.

"The town's full of foreigners," Tom went on. "Didn't you see in the paper tonight what I read you?"

"Well, Mr. James will certainly not fight a duel," she said. "It's against the law."

"Do you think they'll give him much choice, and them with the pistols?"

"We're in America, boy. Not in the wilds of . . . (God help her, she had almost said Ireland) . . . Russia."

"What do you propose to do then?" Tom cried. "Write him a message and go to bed?"

"I propose to wait up for him," Mrs. Norris said, "as I have on more nights than you've seen daylight after."

Tom straightened up and squared his shoulders to the utmost limits of the damned silk coat. He took it off then, and perhaps forever. "I propose to set him on guard—*en guarde!* I'm going out now and find him. You might say a prayer."

"I'll get my hat and meet you in the garage," Mrs. Norris said.

"You're a woman, not a detective," the young Irishman said in his first and last attempt to put her in her place.

Mrs. Norris pulled a full measure of Victorian dignity out of her dumpy shape. "I've had sufficient experience in both categories to qualify," she said. "I'm going with you."

10

Jimmie returned completely frustrated to the ballroom where Helene was waiting for him. D'Inde rubbed his hands together and made what Jimmie assumed were solicitous noises when he said that Senator Fagan had gone. Jimmie regretted it immediately, but he turned on the Frenchman: "Are you inoculated against this sort of thing?"

"I do not understand."

"Weren't you at the Chatterton dinner party?"

"Oh, yes. Ai! I suppose that's the significance of Madame's fainting, eh? What the senator said in the paper tonight?"

"It would seem like a fair deduction," Jimmie said.

"Now I understand your question," the Frenchman said. "And I am not immune. After all, I am an alien."

"Sorry I said that," Jimmie murmured. "I'm concerned about my father."

The Frenchman shrugged. "All they can do to me, I think, if I am associating with bad company—they can deport me. But the General, they cannot very well deport him, can they?"

The apparent acquiescence to Fagan on all sides aggravated the very devil out of Jimmie. After all, everybody at the Chatterton dinner could not be vulnerable.

"Perhaps not," Jimmie said, "but they can hold up his pension—and his good name to ridicule," which he thought grimly, his father could do without Fagan's assistance. Then he exploded, "What nonsense this is, talking this way!"

"I agree," Helene said. "I've never seen you—hamstrung before."

The Frenchman was looking at him speculatively, calculating his politics, his vulnerability. That was the deadly game Fagan set in motion: Russian roulette could scarcely be worse.

"The worst thing about it all," Jimmie said, "so much is beyond the reach of law, and so much beneath the law . . ."

"And the senator, of course, above the law," Helene said.

"Exactly," said Jimmie and the Frenchman nodded. They seemed to have become a triangle. But Jimmie had begun to feel more composed. "Do you know Chatterton well, Dr. d'Inde?"

"I know Mrs. Chatterton. She is an art patron. Very generous woman."

Jimmie then asked a direct question, something Mrs. Norris had trained him from childhood to avoid as bad manners. "Do you know the woman with whom my father left the dinner?"

D'Inde cocked his head wistfully. "I cannot know every woman, much as I should like to be able to." No one had trained him in direct answers at any rate.

Helene smiled apparently charmed. Jimmie thought him as charming as a jackdaw.

"If you will excuse me a moment," he said, "I am going to call home. It's just possible they will have heard from Father."

Jimmie phoned from the lounge. It was a long chance indeed, he mused, listening to the telephone signal. He wondered if his father, wherever he was, had heard the news of Fagan's charge. Chatterton was a friend of his . . . A strange assortment of people for him to have gathered regardless of Fagan's charges: d'Inde made sense, but was there no Madame d'Inde? Or was she home with the brood, obliging some ancient Gallic tradition? The violinist, Katz: he was an ageing prodigy, not first rate by any means although his concert was sold out. Jimmie happened to know that the concert had been lately arranged, to coincide with the Beaux Arts Ball Week, and Katz was the best available performer. Maria Candido: he seemed to recall that her reputation as a singer of bawdy songs far outdistanced her operatic fame. The whole party was damned indiscreet of Chatterton, bad taste, and quite out of character. If Cabinet Secretary Jennings was involved in anything scandalous—that was unthinkable, really; one of *the* daughters of the country—but if she were involved, the administration was involved. Probably what

Fagan wanted. The man couldn't stand to be tolerated: he wanted either to be kicked out like a bum or proposed as a presidential candidate.

Jimmie realized then that the phone had been ringing for a long time. He broke the connection and then called again, to be sure it had not been a wrong number ringing. There was no answer. This, on top of everything else, was very distressing. Mrs. Norris was most unlikely to go out her first night in Washington. Of one thing, he was sure: she would have left a message for him at home. When he could no longer rely on Mrs. Norris, Jimmie thought, he would consider it folly for the human race to continue propagating itself.

When he returned to the ballroom, d'Inde volunteered gallantly to see Helene home if M. Jarvis felt it imperative to leave.

The lesser of two imperatives, Jimmie thought, choosing to go home now. He gave the Frenchman dry thanks and then asked, "If you don't mind, Dr. d'Inde, can you tell me again who the other men at the dinner were?"

"I did not pay very much attention, but I will try—ah, Ambassador Cru. Do you know him? No matter, he and Madame Cru. And somebody I think called Montaigne— a young man. He was very gay, and most reactionary. The violinist, M. Katz, who was very melancholy. And that is all, except the host—and your father, who was, if you don't mind me saying it, also very gay."

He didn't mind d'Inde's saying it half so much as he minded the old man's being it. "Forgive me for not seeing you home,

Helene?" He was more than a little hurt that she did not insist on accompanying him.

She put her hand in his and clung to it for a second. "Call me . . . or come," she said in a voice not quite a whisper but intended for him only to hear. There was, he became aware, some purpose to her easy consent to d'Inde's escort. "I do understand, of course," she said more loudly.

"By the way, Jarvis," the Frenchman said, "your father had words with that Montaigne boy—as I did myself."

"On politics?"

"On Hitler and Mussolini. Of course, I suppose you could call it politics."

"Oh," Jimmie said, relieved. His father was rather fond of talking about the Russians. He liked to say that some of his best friends were Russians. Whereupon he often recited their names, making up some of them, Jimmie was sure, for rhyme and metre. What it did for the Russians at home, friendship with an American army officer, Jimmie used sometimes to ponder, little realizing until the last few months how little it might prosper the American at home.

Montaigne, Jimmie thought, awaiting the delivery of his car: he did not suppose he had ever heard the name except for the sixteenth century French essayist.

In the car Jimmie turned on the radio as he headed along the Potomac. It was time for the 12.30 news. He did not know whether or not he really wanted to hear it. Surely there were other important things going on in the world. There were, but Jimmie soon discovered he was not listening to them: he was waiting for the name, Senator Fagan, convinced he would hear it before the broadcast was over. How many throughout the city were waiting for the same thing, albeit less intimately concerned: there were some people to whom Fagan's revelations had more suspense than a lottery. And the senator never failed his public. The newscaster said:

"A late bulletin. Reached by telephone within the hour. Senator Fagan announced that tomorrow morning he would turn over to the proper authorities for investigation the names of persons involved in tonight's charges. Earlier, the mid-western lawmaker had accused a prominent member of the State Department of entertaining at least four known subversives . . ."

Jimmie switched off the radio and turned into his own driveway. The garage was empty. Even Tom's jalopy was gone. He knew the moment he let himself in the house that the only possible company he might find there was the family cat, and he thought bitterly, observing her reluctant rise from the kitchen rocker at his approach, she wouldn't be home either if she weren't already pregnant.

Not a note anywhere: it was entirely unlike Mrs. Norris. Of course, she might have been persuaded earlier to go riding with Tom, and something might have happened to delay them; almost anything could happen in his automobile; he called it "Sophie" in honour of a singer of comparable vintage.

Then the cat jumped up on the table, a laborious leap; but thus was Jimmie's eye attracted to the words Mrs. Norris had written as Tom remembered them: "Key Bridge, Arlington side," and the card on which was engraved the name, "Leo Montaigne."

Jimmie sat down for a moment and made a lap for the cat. The handwriting was Mrs. Norris', no doubt of it. But the card, Leo Montaigne's—what was it doing here? Had his father been home? What had gone on here that had taken Tom and Mrs. Norris from the house? The cat stretched and began to purr and knead her paws. Her claws went through to his flesh.

Jimmie thought then of Virginia Allan, remembering her name. She was the woman with whom he presumed his father to be right now. And Virginia Allan sang at a club, or so Helene had said. He got up and put the cat in the chair. He phoned Helene's hotel and left the message to have her call him here as soon as she came in. Then he sat down to think and wait, staring at the engraved card. It was obvious now that his father was more deeply involved than as a chance dinner guest at Chatterton's.

It suddenly occurred to him to wonder where Helene had learned Virginia Allan sang blues at a club. He remembered the words, for he had proposed to think she might be a ballad singer. Where but from Henri d'Inde?

But in answer to Jimmie's question, d'Inde had declined to acknowledge that he knew the singer. On grounds that it might tend to incriminate him?

Jimmie lit a cigarette and began to pace the kitchen while the cat miaowed.

11

Mrs. Norris had not ridden in anything like "Sophie" since Master Jamie had mounted an orange crate on roller skates and persuaded her into it. She clung now to her hat with one hand and to the door handle with the other.

"What kind of a car is it?" she asked at the top of her voice.

"As near as I can figure, she's half-Ford and half-Chevrolet," Tom shouted.

Mrs. Norris sat back, more or less. She was glad she had worn sensible shoes: there was no telling from where she might have to walk home. Not, of course, that she could find "home" if she were across the street from it. Nyack was never like this.

Tom drove directly up to the hotel entrance. He tumbled out and ran for the building without a word.

The doorman shouted after him, "Come back here! You can't leave a can like that in front of the door."

"The lady'll explain everything," said Tom, and disappeared.

The doorman came to the car window. He had the decency to remove his cap at least before sticking his face into Mrs. Norris'. "Can you drive this contraption?"

"I might if I was wearing spurs," Mrs. Norris said, and there was a burr to her spur.

The doorman pulled out. "Are you looking for someone?"

"We are. For Congressman Jarvis who is here at the ball."

"Jarvis, did you say?"

"I did."

"He's just left. I called up for his car not ten minutes ago."

Tom came out at a gallop and leaped in beside Mrs. Norris. The car seemed almost alive to his touch. It was very nearly beautiful, she thought, the grace with which he could manoeuvre something so ugly. He dimmed the lights and nosed Sophie around a curb and into position.

"This way, if we have to, we can take off in any direction," he explained.

"We'll be fortunate if it's not in all of them," Mrs. Norris said over the rattle of her teeth. "Mr. James has left. Or did you find that out yourself?"

"I deducted it," said Tom. "Herself will be coming out in a minute with the Frenchman."

"Mrs. Joyce?"

"The same, cruel vixen that she is. We're going to shadow them."

"In this?" said Mrs. Norris.

"Why not?" said Tom. "She can do everything but climb a tree, Sophie can."

Mrs. Norris would not have been surprised to see her climb a tree. She laid a hand on Tom's wrist; it was tense and sinewy, his hand tight on the wheel. "Why did this man send the message to the house, Tom, and both him and Mr. James here all the time? It's only a minute or two since Mr. James left, the doorman says. I think you're making it all up, just to get out on a lark."

"A great lark, with you along clipping my wings. There they are, getting into that cab!" Tom eased the car into first gear and allowed it to roll gently forward.

Mrs. Norris, peering at the couple, and at her mind's after-image of them when they were out of view, knew that if it was Mrs. Joyce in the cab, she was not there with Representative Jarvis: and that in itself portended trouble, so she held her peace.

Tom had no trouble following the cab to the hotel where he said Mrs. Joyce was stopping.

"I hope she doesn't invite him up," Mrs. Norris said without realizing she had said aloud her moral appraisal of the situation. For Mr. James' sake she wanted fervently to believe in Mrs. Joyce.

"So do I," said Tom, but for quite another reason. "Oh, we're in luck. He's having the cab wait."

"You're going to follow him from here?"

"Sure, as long as we're on his tail, he's not fighting with the boss, is he?"

"I'd rather, to tell you the truth, be following Mr. James."

"That wouldn't even be decent," Tom said. He let the car motor idle lower. "What kind of shoes do you have on in case we have to go after him on foot?"

"They're as good as my feet," she said. "Isn't that him now?" The man came out of the hotel at a much faster pace than he had gone in. Truly he seemed to stride with purpose and Mrs. Norris' heart gave a leap in spite of herself.

"Look sharp, Sophie," Tom said. The cab shot ahead and then left a smokescreen as the driver changed speeds. "He's in earnest now, wherever he's going. By God, I hope the old girl doesn't backfire! She'd give us away sure, and us the only ones on the road. Sophie, behave, dear!"

"You'll soon have company at this speed, if there are police," Mrs. Norris said. She could make neither head nor tail, north nor south of the Washington streets, the names of which she was no sooner finding than she was losing. It was a town put together in diamond patches, like a quilt designed from the centre.

"Where are we now?" she asked, not that she would know, being told.

"In the neighbourhood of Dupont Circle. I've a notion he'll stop here. It's an artisty kind of section."

Tom's hunch was right. The cab came to a sudden stop and he had to take Sophie around it. It was to be said for his boldness, he did it with a flair, giving a blast of his horn to the cabbie for not having warned him of the sudden stop.

"Baaaa," said the cabbie, articulate as a goat.

"Sounds just like New York," Mrs. Norris said.

"Watch where he goes in," Tom alerted her.

"I didn't come only for the ride," Mrs. Norris said. "He's already in and I've seen where he went." She was grateful for the moonlight, and drew her identification of the house from a tree stump.

Tom drove around the block and parked near the corner. "I wonder if he's come home for the artillery."

"The what?"

"Pistols. What he wants to fight with. Come on and show me the house. We'll walk by."

There wasn't a sound but their own footfalls and the burble of frogs, as they went silently toward the tree stump Mrs. Norris had chosen as marker. Then there were other sounds—music of a listening variety somewhere nearby, and laughter from somewhere else, the distant banging of a car door, a dog's barking.

"There it is," Mrs. Norris said, indicating a two-family stone dwelling.

"We're all right if he lives in the one on the left," said Tom. "The blinds are up, and there's people you can see through to." The other half of the house was in darkness.

"You've the eyes of a ferret," she said, but yielded her hand to his when he groped for it, and allowed herself to be led off the sidewalk into the shadow of bushes near the house. "We're trespassing, Tom."

"Aye, and I wonder if he isn't himself. Look there, he's talking to some woman with a baby in her arms."

"I can't see a thing," Mrs. Norris said, for the window was above a veranda.

"Well, I'm not going to lift you up," said Tom. "You'll have to take my word for it."

The room to the front of the house was dark, but Mrs. Norris could see the shadows from the figures in the second room playing upon the ceiling. Suddenly the woman was trying to thrust the baby into the man's arms, and he was backing away from it, his own arms flailing while he talked.

"The bloody villain," said Tom in a hoarse whisper. "He won't take it from her. No wonder the women are stepping on us every chance they get. Whisst! Here he comes."

Mrs. Norris gave Tom a poke and pointed to the open window nearby. The Frenchman's voice came out to them clearly, but alas, he was speaking in a foreign language, presumably French.

"What's he saying?" said Tom into her ear.

"I think he's crying," said Mrs. Norris, for the tone much suggested it. She also caught the word "petit". The man then lit the lamp and began to gather papers out of a desk. Mrs. Norris took a chance with the possibilities. "I think he's getting ready to leave, and he doesn't want to go at all."

Tom nodded, his mouth a bit open, she presumed in admiration of her knowledge of French.

The woman came into the room without the baby, and the man took her into his arms. She was an ample body, Mrs. Norris thought, overflowing him by a few pounds. Between the tears and the gestures, and the foreign language, the scene bore a remarkable resemblance to grand opera.

"I'll go up and pack your suitcase," the woman said then in a native American voice.

"Do not wake the children," he cried after her dramatically. "I could not bear any more adieus tonight."

Tom and Mrs. Norris nodded at one another, having heard the confirmation. In the house, the instant the woman had gone upstairs, the Frenchman came to the windows and drew the shades, a great precision about his movements. A few seconds later—before the watchers had decided on their next move—he came out into the vestibule in his shirtsleeves and, most curiously, worked at the mailbox. He seemed to be removing or changing the nameplate.

As soon as he returned to the living room, Tom skipped lightly into the vestibule, glanced at the boxes on both sides and came out, all in a few seconds.

"He's taken the nameplate off," he whispered. He caught Mrs. Norris' arm and led her a distance from the house. "The name of the people on the other side is Walker, by the way. You know—the whisky?

"I thought you didn't drink," Mrs. Norris said.

"There's no harm, is there, in knowing what I'm missing?" Tom snapped. "I want to go round now and see if he has a car in a garage. I'll be back in a minute. Keep watch."

Mrs. Norris had never in her life minded the darkness, and she had certainly long since become used to no company but her own. But it was a curious thing she was doing just now, standing on one foot and then the other, spying on an utter stranger in Washington, D.C., and with no other justification than the say-so of a wild young Irishman with the Gaelic imagination. The more she thought about it—and it was a long, long minute he was gone—the madder she thought the whole business. Nonetheless, she made a note of her surroundings, the number of the house, and then the hour of the night. It was 12.40.

Within the house a child started to cry, and then, if she was not mistaken, another. It sounded like a whole parcel of them. And still Tom did not return. The front door of the house opened and the Frenchman came out, dressed now in a business suit, and walked briskly across the veranda to within a foot or two of the very spot Tom and Mrs. Norris had been standing a few minutes before. Without wasting a motion, he removed the round head from one of the balusters in the veranda rail, put his hand into the hollow and drew out a small, oblong parcel. He replaced the head, and then, about to go indoors again, paused and closed the window, cutting off the sound of the squalling from within.

Mrs. Norris knew then that Tom, whether in spite or because of himself, was onto something. The Frenchman hurried indoors. From down the street, someone was whistling. She listened a second: *Annie Laurie.* She went to the sidewalk and looked. Tom was leaning against a lamp post. He straightened up when she came into sight, gave a little jerk of his head and ambled toward Sophie. He had doubtless seen every movie John Ford ever made. Mrs. Norris paced herself unhurriedly, and joined him in the car.

"We'll wait for him here," said Tom. "He has to come out by this way if he takes the car. And if he calls a cab, we can't chance being seen on the walk when it comes for him."

"Indeed we can't," said Mrs. Norris. "Not after what I've just seen." She told him of the baluster with the removable head.

Tom listened, his eyes shimmering like stars in a teacup. "Oh," he said in almost profound ecstasy. "Aren't we going to have a time!"

12

Jimmie had had to wait for Helene's call only a few minutes, but it seemed much longer in the big house alone. For this he had brought Mrs. Norris to Washington! And hired Hennessy! And proposed a home for his father!

When Helene's call did come, she could tell him nothing more than he had already surmised: her information came from d'Inde. But she said, "Jimmie, come over here. I may have information by the time you get here, and I think it's just as well to avoid an hotel phone. Don't you?"

Jimmie arrived to find Senator Grace Chisholm waiting at the elevator. They went up to Helene's suite together, both, Jimmie was sure, measuring one another in terms of sense and sensibility. In the apartment, the senator threw off her velvet wrap somewhat as she might a buffalo robe, and came to the point immediately.

"I assume I am not interrupting a sociable evening here?"

"My father has managed to take so much of the sociability out of my life," Jimmie said, "I sometimes envy the frolics in a monastery."

"That tells me something of what I want to know," the senator said. She turned to Helene. "Mrs. Joyce, how well do you know this d'Inde man?"

"That would tell me something I want to know, too," Jimmie said dryly.

"Well enough only to concur in most of his opinions about sculpture," Helene said.

"Is he *bona fide*?" the senator asked.

"I should think it would be better to ask that of the director of the Museum," Helene said.

"I intend to, but not at one in the morning, and now is when I want to know."

"I feel that he knows his business," Helen said. "I have had correspondence with him and I've met him two or three times. I will admit to a small prejudice in that he likes my work."

The senator turned to Jimmie: "Do you know why your father was invited to Chatterton's tonight?"

"I assumed it was because they are friends," Jimmie said, "but I'd certainly like to know why some of the other guests were there."

Grace Chisholm nodded. "The oddest pack outside of a

zoo. I think your father and I are in a mess, Congressman, and since, to tell you the truth, I thought he was being played for a fool at dinner tonight, I'm in danger of being a mite righteous. But I don't know why *I* was invited to the Chatterton table tonight."

"Why did you go then?" Jimmie asked quietly.

The older woman looked at Helene and smiled. "He asks because he doesn't know, doesn't he?" Helene nodded. The senator went on: "Vanity, young man. Plain and simple, that's it: I was flattered to be asked by so urbane a gentleman."

"Then you and Chatterton had met?"

"Only on the same terms as he would have met two or three dozen other people on the Hill. I don't see any way of figuring out this mess if we don't tell the truth when we see it. I think I can fairly say I wasn't there because of friendship."

"Whom did you know among the other guests, Senator?"

"General Jarvis, Secretary Jennings, and I'd met this d'Inde fellow before."

"That adds up to four, doesn't it?" Jimmie said.

"Simple arithmetic," the senator said. "Even Fagan's kind."

"Well, I don't think we should do it for him, do you?" Jimmie said. "But we must assume he has some foundation, whatever it is, and however it came about."

"Agreed."

"What about Dr. d'Inde?" Helene said. "You came here because you thought I knew him, didn't you, Senator?"

"And because I knew this young man was likely to be

concerned with the same problem I was, the disloyalty charges Fagan has aimed at the Chatterton dinner."

Jimmie was impatient, but he tried to hold steady: piece by piece. "Something has made you genuinely suspicious of d'Inde, however," he suggested.

"Could be entirely irrelevant," Senator Chisholm said, "but it came back to me tonight. I was coming out of a committee meeting one day last week—an Armed Forces Planning hearing where we'd been shown some pretty top secret stuff. D'Inde bottled me up and tried to get me to look at some photostats he had, thought I'd find them interesting. I gave him the brush the same way I would newspaper men on the subject. I make it an absolute practice never to talk of what goes on in those meetings outside."

"How did he react?"

"Formal, polite. 'But of course, Madame Senator—I understand.' And he was nice as pie at the Chattertons."

"Did you see the photostats?"

"Well, sort of the way you see the countryside from a train window. I saw geometric drawings and math figures. I couldn't see more, refusing to look."

"He wasn't exactly covert about it, though," Jimmie said.

"Not in the least. And maybe you can tell me, Congressman, if that's good or bad."

Jimmie grinned. "I know what you mean. Imagination and timing: most factors are alterable."

"Exactly. A white dress makes a black shadow."

Jimmie's respect for this grey-haired, blunt woman had

deepened considerably. He drew the engraved card from his pocket and gave it to her.

"Leo Montaigne," she said. "I sat next to him at dinner. Do you know him?"

Jimmie shook his head. "But when I went home tonight, I found this card on the kitchen table—and nobody at home; not my housekeeper, my man, and certainly not my father. Mrs. Norris had written the words 'Key Bridge, Arlington side' on the table, but I don't even know that there is any connection. I came back by way of the Key Bridge. Nothing."

"He can't be more than thirty," the senator said, "but he smells musty, talks about the Riviera. He didn't have much to say to me, but he seemed on intimate terms with the rest of the crowd."

"All of them?" Jimmie queried.

"No, I wouldn't say that. He had an argument with d'Inde. Your father took d'Inde's side, I think. But it was trivial. I'm sure of that. Oh, something that struck me as queer; he was sitting between me and Secretary Jennings, and do you know, he called her by her first name?"

"Curious," Jimmie agreed, but there was something else curious, too. He was looking at the list of guests he had compiled with d'Inde's help. "Have you any idea what he does for a living?"

"Yes. And come to think of it, I found out by eavesdropping on the conversation across the table—between General Jarvis and whatever her name was. Montaigne runs something called the Club Sentimentale, and this woman is supposed to sing there."

Jimmie got up. "Well, as they used to say in the D.A.'s office, somebody sang tonight. I think I'll try the Club Sentimentale."

"Senator Chisholm, will you stay and have some coffee with me?" Helene said.

"Bless you, girl, I will."

Jimmie took his hat. Helene went out to the deserted hall with him and, when he gently lifted her chin with his fore-finger, kissed him as though it were going to have to last him for some time.

"I'd almost forgotten there were moments like this," he said.

Helene said, "There aren't. You have to steal them. Call me as soon as you can."

13

There were no more than a half-dozen private automobiles scattered along the street near the Club Sentimentale. Washington was a city of taxicabs. Sometimes Jimmie thought its economy was structured on the zoning of cab fares. Certainly the economy of government employees was. Jimmie parked his car.

The music reaching his ears was peculiarly thin, reedy, although the beat was ragtime. An electrified carriage lamp hung at the side of the club door, one weak light bulb faintly illuminating the sign. Identification, not advertising, he thought. The building itself was like an old stable, or perhaps a dock shed. There was even the suggestion of motion, but that doubtless was due to the ripple of moonlight on the Potomac in the background. It was an eerie night, at least down here: there was much so-called postwar building under way in this area, and everywhere the night-stilled cranes, derricks and other monsters of construction stood gaunt and fearsome as some nameless survivors of a dead era. About them, too, there was a suggestion of motion: and that, Jimmie realized, was the wafting of light clouds in the sky above them. A solitary cab was parked in the hackstand, driverless.

Jimmie opened the heavy door and went inside, ignoring the jangling bell that reacted to the door's motion. A bar stood some distance in front of him, he thought, although it would have been better lit by pure moonlight. The music was still off somewhere like an auditory will-o'-the-wisp. He stood just inside the door, trying to accustom his eyes to the atmosphere. He sensed walls close on either side of him. Catching the scent of disinfectant he supposed the washrooms were on his left.

Someone spoke to him from out of the darkness on his right. "Are you a member of the Sentimentale, sir?" The female voice was jazzy, coming from false tones, he would guess, deliberately off-key.

Jimmie also guessed that he had been thoroughly observed in the few seconds by someone better accustomed to the semidarkness. He ventured to move a few steps forward. "No, I'm not. But I come well recommended. I should like to see Mr. Montaigne, please."

She flipped over her hand so that its palm was upturned. "Let me have your hat."

Jimmie, seeing better now, at least as far as he was looking, watched her sashay into the cloakroom and out again. She gave him a tab for his hat and then, hips swaying, led him into the bar-room and through it into the main clubroom. Her hair was blonde-white, glittery with some sort of luminous dust. The top of her dress was V'd, back and front, and fit her snugly but without a waistline all the way to the hips where it ruffled out into an extremely short skirt. He was put in mind of the frilled panties worn by the well-turned-out lamb chop. She might have been done up, Jimmie thought, for a Warner Baxter movie.

And then he knew, of course, what there was about the entire place that made it dreamlike: it was a reconstructed speakeasy, a club of the 'twenties, which Jimmie could best identify from the midnight films on television. Sitting down at the red-checked cloth and looking round at the half-curtains hung on shuttered windows, he got the feeling of being on a movie set.

"I'll tell Leo you want to see him," the hostess said. "Do you want a little drink?"

"Could I have a Scotch and soda?" Jimmie asked, not sure that such a drink was in order here.

The blonde gave his shoulder a gentle "go-on-with-you" sort of push. "Sure. Leo's got anything you want."

Something ticklish ran down Jimmie's spine. The orchestra was playing *It Happened in Monterey . . . a long time ago.* There was a patch of dance floor in the middle of the room, but no one danced. There were maybe twenty people present, all of them bent a little forward in their seats toward the orchestra, the only variation in their attitude, the hands under some chins. Jimmie began to feel himself misplaced, an anachronism.

Leo, Jimmie thought; it was not exactly a common name, except perhaps among popes.

The orchestra—three pieces, a shoofly drum, a saxophone and a piano—finished *Monterey*. While the musicians tuned up, a faint murmur of conversation ran among the guests—or members. The lights on all the tables were heavily shaded so that Jimmie saw most people in silhouette only; nonetheless, he sensed a familiarity about two or three of them. This too made him feel uneasy about time and place, for certainly no one of his acquaintance was likely to be here—except possibly his father and he had not spotted him yet. And in truth, this place was not at all likely to be to his father's tastes. The old boy did not live in the past, alas.

The hostess brought his Scotch and soda—already mixed. There was not a great deal of drinking done here, Jimmie thought, if she could handle it. The customers came for some other sort of soporific.

The hostess waited until Jimmie had taken a sip. "Okay?"

"Thank you, it's fine." It was not exactly fine, but it wasn't dreadful either.

"Leo's busy till after the show," she said. "What's your name?"

"James," Jimmie said, reluctant to disturb his incognito.

And that reminded him of Mrs. Norris. Where was she? Had she been here? After all, she had taken some sort of message about or by Montaigne. "Have you seen a woman here tonight, not a member—oh, getting on toward sixty, roundish, looks a bit like Queen Victoria?"

"Can't you tell me her name? I wouldn't want to commit myself on another woman's looks."

Jimmie saw no harm in giving it. "Mrs. Norris."

The blonde shook her head.

"What about a strapping young Irishman, good looking, in his early twenties?"

The blonde gave a wiggle that ran from her head to her toes. "Uhn-unh, but you send him along any time. I'd love to entertain him."

Jimmie pulled his neck a little higher out of his collar. Most of the table lamps went out then, a master switch apparently, and a spotlight flooded the dance floor. A young man came out from behind the orchestra and down through the watchers, getting a flourish of applause as a welcome. He wore a tophat and carried a cane, and when he took off the hat, his hair was brushed back, sandy and sleek.

"Welcome sinners . . ." The applause to this beginning was perfunctory. "Well, we can't all, all the time, can we? . . . Just the same wasn't it a busy day in Washington? I'm glad so many of us are gathered here together. Some, I hear, have fled to the woods. The redcoats again. I don't think they've ever gone home, myself. I was just thinking about that a little while ago, and I said to myself, all right—let them stay. They can have Washington. I'll take Paris. Anybody else want to go to Paris tonight?"

It was fascinating, Jimmie thought, the way all these faces had turned up as to the sun. A great chorus of yeas and hurrays rang out an answer to the question the M.C. had just asked. Everybody wanted to go to Paris. He began pouring on the nostalgia then. It was better than reading Elliot Paul. And in this Paris of his, there walked yet and much alive, the long dead, Joyce and Scott Fitzgerald, Grace Moore, George Gershwin, quite as gracefully as though their future had never passed.

He told his tale in the exhortation of an evangelist, and some people there found Paris. There were happy tears in their eyes. Jimmie began himself to dread the moment Montaigne would break the spell. The return to reality must be very harsh. It was then ten after one; at one-thirty Montaigne was telling anecdotes still, and much as though they flowed from recent memory, memory as detailed as the prose of Marcel Proust.

Jimmie remembered then d'Inde's remark about Montaigne—very gay but reactionary, and there were words about Mussolini and Hitler between him and the General. Such names would spoil his séance, like a dead cat tossed into a banquet. And yet, not necessarily. The world he was recreating would acknowledge the dictators only in their early promise, not their grim fulfilment. Montaigne might even affect an admiration for Mussolini, as a number of young men did, sojourning in Italy in those days.

Jimmie was caught up in admiration despite his first and deep revulsion. Young Montaigne had the imagination

93

of genius. He had actually brought to life a dead world and closed out the living present. He had, for as long as he regaled them, taken twenty-five years from the lives of each member of his cult. How often, Jimmie wondered, could he do this? Was tonight a very special occasion? Jimmie doubted that one of such imagination could stand self-repetition indefinitely. Then what? And how did he come by this depth of verisimilitude? Not merely out of books, off films. Jimmie would suspect there was a real live model—perhaps clinging to a lost youth of her own by making him her lover . . . Speculation, yes. Virginia Allan? Then what was she doing with Father?

Suddenly it was over. A stillness and a limpness pervaded the room, the people hangdog. No applause. Gloom. Montaigne himself stood, his head lolling forward, his long hair streaming over his face, his arms dangling. It might have been the awed moment after a magnificent orchestral performance, and he the conductor. And in a way it had been just that.

Someone at a table nearby sobbed. There had been an attempt to stifle it, but the sound of repressed emotion escaped.

Montaigne lifted his head and threw back the hair from his face. "No tears tonight!" he cried out. "I promise you the night has just begun. Stay with me, friends, and watch. Your vigil will have its own reward. Now!" He threw back his shoulders and rubbed his hands together.

"Now. In the absence tonight of our dear old Virginny . . ."

"No! No!"

"We want Virginia!"

"Virginia Allan!"

There was an increasingly vigorous protest from the audience. Montaigne seemed to lose his temper.

"I tell you she is not here! She ran off tonight with an Army man. . . ."

Someone tittered. Montaigne screamed, "It isn't funny at all, you fools!"

Some woman in the audience made a soothing noise, as she would perhaps to a child. Jimmie could feel the sweat break out on his back.

Montaigne threw his head back and gave a violent direction of his arm, pointing to the orchestra. "Play, you clowns! Dolores, come out here and sing!"

He half-walked, half-glided then among the tables and off to the room behind the orchestra, never pausing an instant and rejecting all the hands of women flung out to him as he passed. Jimmie started to get up, intending to confront him at once.

The hostess, behind him, put her hand on his shoulder. "Not now."

"When?"

"After Dolores gets off. Wouldn't you like another of those?" She indicated his drink.

"All right," Jimmie said, but resolved not to drink it. He waited until the woman was out of sight, intending then to make his own way to Montaigne. Dolores was singing, something inane and in a voice he could only think of as dollish. Even he could tell she was phony. No umph. Jimmie had passed but a few tables when he stopped and sat down at the next empty one. Montaigne was at the door, smoking, watching Dolores through the smoke with an intentness Jimmie had rarely known in anyone who wasn't in love.

Although Montaigne himself led the applause the rest of it was only perfunctory. Jimmie took a good look at Dolores as she left the floor. She might not have nostalgia, he thought, nor "it", nor "umph", and she might not fit the 'twenties' makeup someone had plastered on her, but she had one thing in common with Leo Montaigne that so far as Jimmie had observed no one else in the house shared: she too was very young.

14

The General stood, his hands behind his back, before the fireplace in which there was no fire because Miss Virginia Allan was concerned about a bird's nest in the chimney. The wall above the mantel was a virtual arsenal of weapons— shotguns, a rifle, a snub-nosed revolver, a set of pistols, really nasty looking.

"Those are my souvenirs, Ransom," Virginia purred up at him from the sofa.

"Of what, my dear?" The General half-expected her to say of her late husbands.

"My hunts for antiques."

"Not all of them are antique, you know."

"I know. There's one or two I keep workable in case I

need 'em—you know, a woman all alone this way in the wilderness."

The General would not like to have given odds on the times she had been alone in the wilderness.

"Are you a good shot, Ransom?"

"Passable."

Virginia laughed, quite prettily. "I'm only passable myself. Come here, honey."

The General skipped across the room.

"Sit down nice and comfy and I'll fetch you another drink." She was up before he was down so there was little point in protest. But he resolved he had taken his last gambol at her command. It was getting on toward two in the morning, and he had not yet discovered what she was up to. That in itself had become a challenge. He brushed his eyes with his hand. He had better go lightly on the whisky or that would be a challenge, too. He was a man who could drink a great deal—in the right company. But he needed good, solid talk, something to tear apart and shake up while he was drinking. And there was no use deluding himself, he had not come here for intellectual stimulation.

She returned and once more they touched their glasses. "I had to switch you to bourbon, Ransom. I hope you don't mind."

"Whisky," he said profoundly, "is whisky." He had just about had enough.

"Have you ever drunk vodka?"

"I don't like the stuff. False friend."

"Just like the Russians, I daresay."

"Not at all, not at all," the General said. "You make a friend of a Russian and you can't get rid of him. He comes to you and sits with his soul. He brings it to you like—a pomegranate, breaks it open in front of you and expects you to sit and pick at it with him."

"I've never had a pomegranate," Virginia said.

The General took a great gulp of whisky to avoid saying what was on his tongue.

"Tell me some more about the Russians. Where did you get to know them, Ransom? You've been just everywhere."

"Oh, I wouldn't say that." He lifted one eyebrow in self-mockery.

She wrinkled her nose at him and laid her hand in his. "Go on."

"I never knew a Russian half as interesting as you, Virginia," he lied out of an old gallantry. "What about this boyfriend of yours—what's his name—Montaigne?"

Just a flicker of what might be malice seemed to have touched her eyes. "Are you interested in him or me, Ransom?"

The General feigned hurt. "Don't you think I could better ask that question at the moment? Did you bring me here to make him jealous?"

She gave a little "ha!" that was quite bitter.

"Is he by any chance going to burst in here and snatch up one of those guns and run me down the hill with it?"

Virginia Allan looked deeply into her glass which he noticed she was holding very tightly. "No, he isn't," she said.

The General reached across and patted her knee. He was beginning to feel paternal. "That's much too bad, isn't it?"

"For somebody," she said, and threw her head back. "I don't want to talk about me, honey. Tell me some more about the Russians. Did you have to negotiate with them?"

"I was part of the American team," he said.

"Can you speak Russian?"

"Nyet."

"Oh, Ransom, you *can*!"

"No, my dear, I cannot."

"What kind of work do you do, Ransom?"

"Ordnance. Supply."

"I don't suppose the Russians would be very interested in that, would they?"

"Not in peacetime, likely."

She smiled at him, "I'm real glad, Ransom."

He looked at her, puzzled.

"A man's honour's more important than his life. At least, that's the southern code, and that's what I live by, Ransom." She seemed on the verge of tears.

"Are you drunk, Virginia?"

"A little, I suppose, honey. Aren't you?"

"No, damn it. I seem to be getting more and more sober."

"It's such a cold world really. Finish your drink and put your arm around me for a minute."

The General threw down the rest of the bourbon, and knew the moment he had done it that it was a mistake. There was just a little taste of bitterness which at the first mouthful he had attributed to the change of whiskies. But now he could see a powdery film on the bottom of the glass. He had been given a powder of some sort. No wonder she was tearful, the witch.

He put the glass down with slow determination. If it were only a sleeping powder, and he assumed that's what it must be, he could, by enormous effort, fight off its taking effect. He had lived too well, too easily these recent years, he thought, and he had taken too much whisky through the evening. The overwhelming temptation was already creeping up on him to put his head on her treacherous little shoulder and let the rest of the world go by.

He sat a moment, his hands dangling between his knees, his head heavy.

"What are you thinking of, Ransom, honey?"

That, little girl, is a great mistake, he thought, to keep me talking. "Oh," he said, fighting the thickness in his mouth, "I was thinking about the time the Soviet *charge d'affaires* offered me a thousand dollars."

"He did?"

The General leaned back on the couch. He was giving a fine imitation, he hoped, of a man about to pass out. Actually he was doing everything but bite his tongue to fight the lure of sleep.

"What for, honey? What'd he give you the thousand dollars for, Ransom?"

"That's a . . . secret," the General said. "But I'll tell you—if you'll tell me a secret. Or aren't you that kind . . . of a woman?"

"I don't understand what you're saying."

"Remember at dinner, my dear—how many years ago?—you said there were some women who couldn't make conversation if they weren't telling secrets?"

"I remember now. But I just don't have any secrets, Ransom."

"You've got lots of them. F'rinstance, why do you want to know my secret?"

"I don't. I just don't really care . . . now." She got up and lit a cigarette.

No more pretence of love-making, no more come-ons, the General thought. She was a little woman in trouble, fighting hard against despair, whatever her game with Ransom Jarvis. She had, of course, lost a young lover—or so it would seem, and there were not likely to be any more of them in her life, not of that age. And a queer duck he was. Social provender.

"Ransom, why don't you just stretch out there and take a little nap? You can go back to town any time before daybreak, can't you? I mean, there's no one waiting up for you, is there?"

"Anyone waiting up for you, my dear?"

"No," she said, and gave a little sob.

"What did you put in my drink, Virginia?"

"Just a little something to make you sleep," she said with disarming directness. "I didn't want you going off and leaving me too soon."

"And why did you want to know about the Russians?"

"Oh, Ransom, it wasn't just the Russians. You don't understand me. I love intrigue, excitement. I wish I was Mata Hari. I'd be a spy right now if anybody'd hire me."

"The trouble with hiring you, my dear—it would be very difficult to tell which side you were on."

"That's very perceptive of you, Ransom. I don't even know, myself."

The General put his head down then and swung his leaden legs up on the sofa. He began counting backwards from a hundred—in Russian. The little lady brought a blanket presently and covered him. He was quite touched when she leaned down and kissed his forehead. "Goodnight, sweet Prince," she said, and he wondered if she did not live in a dream world after all. He went back to the counting in Russian. "Goodnight, sweet Prince," was said in epitaph. He lost count again. Surely she hadn't poisoned him!

Virginia was smoothing out the blanket, tucking it in, apparently, and very close to his pockets. So, deftly, as though trained in the art of pickpocketry, she withdrew the ignition key to the Jaguar from his pocket.

She was a few minutes then putting the room in order, or so it seemed, as she moved about some chore; he dared not move to investigate. She went into the kitchen to wash the glasses, he realized, hearing the tinkle of crystal. He was having less and less trouble fighting sleep now, certainly. But he was fairly reassured that he had not been poisoned, although he did not like to hear her washing glasses.

She started to sing a little tune then, and he relaxed. She was doubtless merely planning to move the Jaguar, perhaps just to see if she could move it. Not a very tuneful voice. But soothing. She would be a great soother. He began to think about her in the altogether—as perhaps a woman he might strike up a permanent liaison with. A little dull, probably, monotonous of voice and far, far too talkative. Too sweet, too talkative, too expensive. . . .

He just caught himself about to drop off when he had thought he was safe from sleep. He began to count furiously against the rhythm of the sudden pounding of his heart. At that moment he heard the Jaguar motor, the scream of gears badly shifted, but shifted nonetheless, and before he had got his legs loose from the blanket, he heard the rev of the motor, acceleration, diminution. Virginia and his car were already halfway down the hill.

15

"You know," Tom said, starting the car and idling the motor, "we ought to make provisions in case we have to split up." They had been watching from the street corner for ten minutes. "For example, what if he's already come out and gone the other way on foot?"

"Nobody goes anywhere on foot in Washington from what I've heard," Mrs. Norris said.

"Aye, 'tis true," said Tom. "They're all beggars on horseback. Still . . . do you think you could drive Sophie?"

"I've never been behind the wheel of a car in my life," Mrs. Norris said, with the air of one who didn't really think it was a woman's place.

Tom was torn between admiration and petulance. "It's a handy thing to know all the same."

"I'd give more right now," Mrs. Norris said, "to know where Mr. James is."

"There!" said Tom. "There's a car coming down the alley. We're off!" Sophie gave a lurch and a shrug. And died. "Oh, my God," said Tom, "I never thought you'd do this to me."

The car he was proposing to follow gave a sudden turn in their direction.

"Down in back of me!" Tom screamed, and he and Mrs. Norris collapsed over one another like a jack and a queen. The headlights of the oncoming car raked them over as the driver took the turn with his tyres squealing, and drove past his own house.

"That was close," Tom said, and stepped on the starter. Sophie caught on immediately. "She must've known," he added reverently, and turned her around in pursuit.

"She has more sense than we have," Mrs. Norris said. "I wouldn't like to crowd him just now anyway."

"I'm going to leave the lights off till we get into traffic," Tom said, "Oh, Lord, don't let me lose him now. Is there a patron saint of detectives, do you know?"

"Are you asking me?"

"Aye, who else?"

"I never heard if there be," Mrs. Norris said, who, herself a good Presbyterian, was not very strong on the saints.

"I dare say St. Anthony'd do. It's him you pray to for something you've lost."

"Well, we haven't lost him yet, thank God," Mrs. Norris said.

Sophie was at least able to keep pace with Tom's prayers and despite the speed, the Frenchman stayed within their vision. Once they almost lost him as Tom looked around driving over a bridge.

"God have mercy, do you know where we are?"

"No. Turn to the left," Mrs. Norris cried.

Tom jerked Sophie around and once again the two small red eyes were visible in the distance. "That was the Key Bridge we just went over," he said. "I was fearful he'd stop."

"I'm glad I didn't know," Mrs. Norris said.

The car ahead, turning into a residential area, mercifully slowed down. He seemed to be trying his lights, or else there was something wrong with them.

"That's a signal," Mrs. Norris said. "He'll be meeting someone or someone will follow him from here."

"We'll make a hell of a sandwich, won't we?" Tom said. "I'm going to drop back a block, in case there's someone waiting for him on a side street."

There was a park to the left, fairly nice spacious homes to the right. Tom braked Sophie. Then he stopped. Far ahead the car they were following had stopped.

"If I can get into the park," said Tom, climbing out of Sophie, "I might get close to him unbeknownst. You stay here, Mrs. Norris, and cover me."

"With what, man?"

"Sophie's horn if you have to. If there's anybody crawling

in behind me you think, give it a touch. But don't bring me back if you don't have to."

"I hope," Mrs. Norris said, "you'll be able to bring yourself back."

She watched him lope across the street and take the park fence with the lightfooted leap of youth. Then she took the measure of the distance between her and the next block. She decided to have a look about for herself on foot. She needed to be a bit closer in any event in order to see. She had reached the age in life where her vision was no longer match for an owl's though once it had been.

Quite elegant houses, really, she observed. Lots of money, and the carelessness typical of America—toys left out, expensive things . . . Ahead of her then, she saw that the man they were following had got out of the car and crossed quickly into the park. Mrs. Norris stood stock still as close as she could get to the trunk of a great tree near the curb. She bent her whole concentration on the sounds and movements of the night. The frogs were still at it here, curdling the silence. No other sound reached her, not even the motors of distant cars, until the running footfalls of Tom. She had not seen the other man return to his car.

She hurried back to the car herself. "I'd swear there was nobody in the park but the two of you," she said.

"Now listen to me," Tom said. "He's in there hiding something in a tree trunk like a bloody squirrel. It might be whatever it was you saw him take out of the post. Do you know where we are?"

"Where?"

"I mean, have you any notion what part of town?"

"None."

"We're in Arlington, no more than a mile or two from the Key Bridge. Would it trouble you terrible to part with me, Mrs. Norris?"

"It wouldn't have troubled me never to have met you," she said. "Say what you have in mind."

"I think one of us should stay here and see who comes for whatever it is he's putting in the tree, and the other of us should keep him in sight. I'm sure that must've been a signal of some sort he gave with the car lights."

"And how am I expected to keep track of whoever it is that comes?"

"You could get their licence number and see if they leave anything in its place. And if I'm alive, I promise to come back here for you."

And, Mrs. Norris thought though it was a bit too grim to say, if she wasn't alive, she'd be here. "What direction is the bridge, did you say?"

He pointed.

"If I have to, I'll try to get there." She was remembering that among the expensive toys so carelessly left outdoors a few houses away was a bicycle. She hadn't been on one in years. But there were a good many things she hadn't done in years, that she would not admit for a moment she was past doing.

"Where's the tree—can you tell me exactly?"

"I can. It's a few feet to the right of the drinking fountain as you go in the park through the gate, and I'll tell you how you'll know it. He's working round the cement plate—the kind a nurseryman puts in to patch up a sick tree, d'you know what I mean?"

"I think so," Mrs. Norris said.

"It shines like a mouthful of teeth in the night."

"He's just come out of the park," Mrs. Norris said, and herself got out of Tom's car.

"You're a brave woman," said Tom.

"Take care yourself, lad, and don't lose him, whatever you do."

"Up the rebels!" Tom cried, and gave Sophie's starter a kick.

As the car ahead pulled out, Tom pulled out, and Mrs. Norris watched the one of them vanish after the other in the night's darkness. She stood by the tree she had begun to consider a friend and waited to be sure no one was in pursuit of them in a car. She crossed the street and entered the park at the first gate, and then took up a position there from which she could watch the patched tree near the fountain.

16

Where, Tom wondered, would a man be going with a suitcase at this hour of the night that he could be followed? Would the Frenchman, having challenged the boss, be getting cold feet now himself? The truth was he wasn't behaving at all like a man who expected to keep an appointment at dawn . . . unless it was the pistols he had packed in the suitcase, and was off right now to await the fatal rendezvous. In that case all the hocus-pocus with the tree and the balusters was his own way of putting affairs in order before going into the fight. There were some people, sure, who had no use for banks. He knew people at home, in fact, who didn't even trust the post office.

But the Frenchman drove over the bridge with nary a puff

of recognition and into Washington again. This time he began working north of M Street. Tom kept on his tail though he wiggled and waggled it, but was very grateful when the route straightened out on Sixteenth Street. He settled Sophie at a steady gait, and began to imagine a chase like this in the daylight: he would need a police escort then to ignore the stoplights, and in his mind's eye he could see the people leaping out of his way and turning after him to gawk in envy. Ah, but wasn't this the country! The only thing you could scatter in his home town in Ireland was a flight of crows.

The realization suddenly came to him that he was a long way from the heart of Washington, and getting farther all the time. It would be a devil of a note if the Frenchman was skipping the country, on his way now maybe to the Canadian border—and Tom with a dollar and fifty cents in his pocket.

Tom pressed his foot down on the accelerator, pushing Sophie up the hill a little faster because the car he followed was now going over the crest. When Tom reached the top himself, there was not a car in sight the whole long street before him.

"Holy, holy, holy," he said aloud, going slowly down the other side that he might peer both ways up cross streets. The Frenchman had vanished, automobile, suitcase and all. "Oh, Sophie, what'll we tell her at all?"

Tom slowly circled the streets, but nowhere did he find the car he had been following. He turned his own car back toward the city and meekly obeyed every traffic light. He longed now to find the boss, which was his first quest anyway, and before facing up to Mrs. Norris, for many a time had the congress-man rescued him from a well-earned folly.

There was no one home, he was sure, driving up. And in the kitchen the only response he got from the cat was a few angry whacks in the air of her tail and the burying of her head into another part of the cushion.

"You're fortunate all that's disturbed is your sleep," he said. But where was the boss?

A plan had been knocking around in the back of his head for the last few blocks home: if the boss had a girlfriend who got him into this mess, sure, the least she could do now was share the anxiety. And the most she could do just possibly, was tell him where the boss was.

"Be bold," he told himself in the words of an Irish proverb, "be ever bold, but be not too bold."

He phoned the hotel and asked for Mrs. Joyce. She answered as though she expected his call.

"Mrs. Joyce, excuse me disturbing you at this hour, but this is Tom Hennessy. Do you know who I am?"

"Mr. Jarvis' man?"

"Aye. Well, it's a long story, but I'm in trouble," he started, and then added hastily, "not on my own account. I wouldn't call you for that, but on account of the boss."

"What's happened?"

"Well, I don't know rightly. I started out to look for him when the challenge came from your French friend. Now mind, I'm not saying you are to blame . . . Oh, Lord, I'm not saying anything right. I'm not saying anything at all."

"On the contrary," Mrs. Joyce said, "Continue. You're saying quite a lot."

"Look, ma'am, it's this way: Mrs. Norris and me started out to look for the boss. Then we thought maybe the Frenchman would lead us to him . . ."

"Dr. d'Inde?"

"What?"

"Tom, in just what way are you in trouble?"

"I'm trying to tell you! After the Frenchman brought you home—I can't say his name so don't make me—but after he brought you home from the ball, he started to act queer, cutting into the house and out of it, hiding things, and then taking off and me trying to follow him. To make a long story short, I just lost him a few minutes ago."

"Where?"

Tom drew a deep breath. He never thought the boss would take up with a stupid woman. "Sure, if I knew that, ma'am, I wouldn't be calling you at all."

"Tom, do you have a car where you are?"

"I do."

"Come right up to the hotel now. I'll leave word you're to be sent up."

And with that she hung up on him. A command performance, no less.

17

Jimmie moved closer to the orchestra by several tables so that he could see the faces of the club's patrons. Dolores might not sing well, but she sang on and on.

What a strange group of people sat as though in a torpor. Middle-aged malcontents, he thought. They were people who did not lack for a certain success in life, for there was the look of prosperity about them, if not of wellbeing: but their success was not enough, or perhaps they had paid too high a price. Something had turned it to ashes. He was reminded curiously of Robert Louis Stevenson's Suicide Club: the bond of the damned.

Jimmie's pulse quickened: he recognized one and then another of Chatterton's dinner guests. Joshua Katz was here, a visitor . . . a guest of a regular? Maria Candido, of course. Jimmie searched his memory for what he knew of Katz: he had been a boy prodigy; that would have been twenty-five years ago, and Jimmie seemed to remember having heard that he was once the spoiled darling of the last royal courts of Europe. He must be a very special catch for this crowd. Candido seemed to be his patroness: perhaps she had been then, too.

Jimmie became aware that he was the object of attention of another lady at that table. She was batting her eyes at him like a mechanized canary—familiar to him but not quite recognizable, as though some vital attribute were missing, a notable husband, perhaps—Latin, attached to some embassy, he decided. He consulted the Chatterton guest list. Of course, Madame and Ambassador Cru. Where was the ambassador?

And where was Father? Gone off with Miss Blues in the night? It was a wise son who knew, Jimmie thought grimly. He bowed slightly to Madame Cru, and ever so gently pulled the chair next to him out from the table by way of invitation.

Madame Cru gathered her purse and gloves. Jimmie wondered if she knew him, or if she was always indiscreet.

"I know you, don't I?" she said, coming up. "Aren't you Ransom Jarvis' son?"

"I am. Madame Cru, I believe?" Jimmie held the chair for her and then sat down beside her.

"We had so counted on your father's joining us here. He's the life of the party, as they say in America."

"They have said it of him in a great many countries besides America, I suspect," Jimmie said.

She looked him over frankly. "You *are* nice-looking. I've been promised you at one of our affairs by a mutual friend."

Dead or alive, Jimmie wondered. "I should be honoured," he murmured, feeling very brittle and not liking it.

A small flurry of applause greeted Dolores' high note. Jimmie and his companion clapped perfunctorily.

"She's not very good, poor child, is she?" The ambassador's wife sighed. "Only very young. Do you know, I shouldn't want to be that young again. Isn't that a strange thing to say? Not . . . in the world out there now anyway." She gave a nod of her dark head to indicate the land beyond the walls of the Club Sentimentale.

Jimmie doubted that he would ever get a better opening. "May I ask, Madame Cru, have you known Montaigne long?"

"We do not speak of time here—not in specific . . . pieces. But then, I forgive you. How would you know our rules? It was in Europe I met him. Elizabeth Jennings was your country's ambassador at The Hague. Leo, you see, is her nephew—if you know what I mean."

Jimmie made a noncommittal noise. He certainly did not know what she meant. But he began to see a pattern in the Chatterton guest list—or at least its link between extremes. "The Jennings are a very well known family," he murmured.

"Really?" Madame Cru smiled unpleasantly. "And which branch of it does he come from, pray?"

"I wouldn't know," said Jimmie, seeing her meaning now.

"No one else seems to either. But then Americans in high places are so loyal—since the days of Andrew Jackson, or even Jefferson—I believe, if the threat of scandal is a woman. If it is merely money, favours, whoosh! it is in every newspaper and on television. But if it is a woman involved, it is a sacred cow, as though all the country would have a moral collapse if a word of it got out. So naïve. You are too many contradictions."

"Better, though, than too many nephews, wouldn't you say?"

She smiled and then made her mouth round with sympathy. "You do not like what I am saying, do you?"

"No," Jimmie said, but amiably.

"And yet it was you who asked the question, and I am not sure it was the question you really wanted to ask at all. You wish to know how a young—what do you call him?—upstart, a saloon-keeper really—receives an invitation to a house like your Under Secretary of State Chatterton's. Am I right?"

"That would have been a more direct question," Jimmie admitted.

"I think I know. But I could not prove it." The ambassador's wife laid her fingers on his wrist for a moment. "You must promise to come to tea and tell me if you find out I am wrong."

"All right," Jimmie said, and smiled as he would to a child or to someone very old who needed humouring.

"Laura Chatterton, you see, is one of us . . . a member of the club. It is so much better than, well, some other things we might be doing, isn't it? No. I don't mean you to answer that. How would you know what it's like to reach the end in the beginning?

"You see, we are a cult, the cult of reality, you might say. All of us, each in his or her own way, discovered one day midlife that we were not going any farther, in fact, that we had already been by very many years at that pinnacle you in America very nicely call 'having arrived'.

"For example, my husband reached the ambassadorial level at the age of twenty-six. It was a wedding present from the president of our country. We have had fourteen presidents since, and my husband has been our chief delegate to fourteen countries. Life has been one long bore."

"Still," Jimmie said, "there are some who would consider the United States an important assignment."

She smiled quite ingratiatingly. "We are Latin American, Mr. Jarvis. In the United States, for us, it is like being very busy in a bottle, in a vacuum—that is the word. Nothing ever happens except the noise we make ourselves."

Jimmie didn't say anything.

Madame Cru continued: "But to talk about Leo. We had all gone past our great moment, you see, and we knew that if we were ever to have anything like its excitement again, we should somehow have to go backwards. Leo taught us that it was possible. He is our guide. He belongs himself in the eighteenth century, he is so very elegant. But he won't admit it. He says not enough people alive now would recognize him. And perhaps he is right. Who knows, they might even think him mad, as he suggests. And he is perfectly at home in that wild decade when all of us were very, very young. Have you understood anything I have told you, Mr. Jarvis?"

"Not everything," Jimmie admitted. "For example, Montaigne himself must have been a child in the early 'twenties."

"I told you—we never think of that. I suppose Virginia Allan is really responsible for his . . . education. Really, I do not enjoy talking this way. It is like taking something exquisite apart: it becomes quite ordinary. It's unfortunate for you, though, that Virginia is not here tonight." Madame Cru cleared her throat delicately. "I think your father may have persuaded her. I hope she doesn't—how shall I say it? Delude him? You see, she and Leo seem to have had a quarrel, but I assure you they are quite inseparable."

"Obviously," Jimmie murmured. "She was at the Chattertons' also."

"Beg pardon?"

Leo himself had come to lead the singer, Dolores, from the spotlight, and all the way to her he applauded, so that a few others of the audience, out of embarrassment perhaps, lent her a hand also.

"She looks genuine, doesn't she?" Jimmie said.

"Yes, but a little too much the flapper, don't you agree?"

Jimmie agreed.

Madame Cru went on: "She does not ring true, like a bad impersonation. Now and then the original comes through, but not enough to keep up the illusion. She doesn't have a heart big enough."

"Only a diamond big as the Ritz," Jimmie murmured.

Madame Cru seemed shocked. "Oh, no."

"It was just a manner of speaking," Jimmie said, somewhat embarrassed. "I was quoting the title of a story."

Madame breathed more easily. "Really it was naughty of your father to have carried Virginia off. It is liable to lead to trouble, or so my husband told me when they did not appear at the ball."

"Is your husband here?" Jimmie inquired.

"No. Something rather important," she said.

"Anything to do with Senator Fagan's allegations about the Chatterton party?"

"I should think not. Our instructions, frankly, are to stay quite clear of Senator Fagan. And my husband always obeys to the letter our government's instructions." The last remark carried the touch of bitterness. Madame shrugged. "I have the imagination in the family or I should not be here, I suppose. At the club, I mean."

"You were going to confide in me, Madame Cru, why you thought Montaigne was welcome at the Chattertons'."

"I was? Yes. Well, now, that does have something to do with Senator Fagan. If I am right, it does. I believe it was through Leo that Madame Secretary Jennings came there to dinner tonight. And it was quite important to Chatterton at this moment in his career to have someone of her influence at, shall we say, his table?"

"Thank you," Jimmie said, and he thought about how much Secretary Jennings must be under the influence of the

121

young nephew. "I take it—since I got in here without any difficulty—the club membership is not secret."

"Certainly not. Anybody is welcome. But we do not talk
about it. How could we explain?" She threw up her hands.
"Impossible!"

"Is Secretary Jennings a member?"

"Of course not. She has just become an officer in your
president's cabinet. That is getting on in the world. You have
not understood what I have told you at all. We are the members of the status quo. Now do you understand?"

Jimmie nodded. "Forgive me. I'm rather in the position of
a non-believer at a church meeting. I would if I could, but I
can't until I'm converted."

The ambassador's wife laid her hand in his for a moment.
"It has been charming talking to you." She looked up. "A
lovely service, Leo." Jimmie also looked up.

Montaigne had almost taken them by surprise, and Jimmie
wondered if that were not his intention. And he had never
before in his life seen eyes quite so fascinating: they fastened
onto a person without seeming to see him at all, as though the
mind behind them was somewhere else. Jimmie would have
sworn at that moment that he was confronting a madman.
The ambassador's wife turned a cheek, and Leo bent to kiss
it, his hair falling over his eyes. He straightened up and threw
his hair back, running his hands over it to settle it in place. He
brought himself into the present to give Jimmie his full attention. "I do not believe we have met."

"I thought perhaps I had just missed you," Jimmie said,

"finding your card in my house." Jimmie showed him the calling card.

Montaigne scarcely glanced at it. His arrogant manner was, to Jimmie, insufferable.

But Madame Cru did not so find him. She was fluttery in his presence. "This is General Jarvis' son," she said, as though eager to account for him as other than her company.

"Indeed? I had thought the old gentleman a bachelor."

Jimmie yielded for the first time to an old temptation in response to so inane a remark: "He is," he said blandly.

"How droll," Montaigne said, smiling. "Are you in government yourself?"

Jimmie quite loathed this elegant fraud. "Not at this moment. I should like an account of why your card awaited me when I got home tonight."

Madame Cru was sidling away from the table. "Don't go, Madame," Montaigne said, and turned back to Jimmie. "As a matter of fact, I am awaiting an account of it myself." He looked at his watch. Jimmie glanced at it. Almost two. "Do you live with your father, Jarvis?"

"We share a house."

Montaigne smiled again. "You have presumed then. That card, dear Jarvis, was presented to your father—or someone acting on his behalf—by my dear friend, Ambassador Cru. I have challenged your father to a duel, come daylight this morning."

"How marvellous!" Madame Cru exclaimed. "Dear Leo, you are magnificent!"

"Leo the magnificent," Jimmie repeated, and sat down. "Well, I'll be damned."

Leo was adjusting his coat sleeves to show the proper length of white cuff.

"Now do you understand, Mr. Jarvis, what I meant by his belonging in the eighteenth century?" Madame Cru said.

Jimmie nodded and sipped some very miserable whisky the blonde hostess just now brought him. It was a publicity gambit, of course, and probably rigged never to come off even if the General could be brought to arms.

The hostess said, "Leo, there's a phone call for you. It's important so you better hurry up."

Montaigne excused himself. "Please don't go, Jarvis. I trust you're a gentleman in an affair like this."

Jimmie did not know for the moment what he would do in either case, acting a gentleman or not acting one. The Key Bridge must be the rendezvous, of course; and whatever else Mrs. Norris heard, she and Tom had taken off with it.

"Your husband's just come in, Madame Cru," the blonde said. "He's got half the newspapermen in Washington with him, it looks like. One of them's even got striped pyjamas on under his suit."

"Probably a zebra," Jimmie said. And in truth, nothing that happened this night would surprise him now.

18

The General splashed cold water on his face and then rubbed his neck with his cold, wet hands. Finally he stuck his head under the kitchen tap. Groping for a towel, he knocked the telephone off its wall cradle.

Thus did it come to his attention. He replaced it and began to wonder if the monotone which he had thought in his stupor to be Virginia singing had not been Virginia on the telephone. The General looked at his watch. It was after two o'clock. Someone must think a very neat plan to be going according to schedule. And wasn't it? The fact that he was conscious instead of unconscious at the moment was small impediment. He had been virtually kidnapped: he was not at all sure, however, that he would like to try to prove it, especially before the court of public opinion where everything seemed to be first tried these days.

But to what purpose was he brought here?

The General was not without resources of his own. He took the phone from the hook. "Let me have the supervisor please."

A few seconds later he said, "I've been trying to put a call through to Washington. I expected the operator to call me back. I wonder if you would be so kind as to check."

"One moment please."

"Right." The General was an old hand at putting just the right tenor in his voice to carry authority.

The operator came on again. "That call was completed, sir."

"Oh?" The General was all apologies. "My wife must have put it through," he improvised with magnificent aplomb. "Have you the number there?"

"Yes, sir," she said, and repeated the number.

"Ah-ha. That's it. I'm sorry to have bothered you." He hung up and waited a long moment. He then called the Washington number.

The moment the receiver was lifted from the hook at the other end, the General knew somebody was having one hell of a party, he felt much relieved.

"Hello out there," a man shouted into the phone at him.

"Who's speaking?" the General demanded.

"Dempsey of the *Post-Citizen*. Who do you want?"

A newspaperman. The reassurance vanished. But the General hesitated only a second. "Listen, Dempsey, I've got a devil of a story for you . . . Where are you now?"

"The Sentimental Club . . . Club Sentimentale. Excuse me, honey child."

"What's going on there?" The General tried again.

"Who the hell are you?" the reporter came back at him.

Ever so gently, General Jarvis broke the connection.

So, he thought, whatever the game was, Virginia Allan was playing it with her boss, her boyfriend. What was it? Conspiracy? Blackmail? She did think he had money, foolish girl. But the truth was, he had not done anything so far that could not have stood photography. And to the best of his knowledge he had not even said anything that the Army Chief of Staff could not have tapped in on. It seemed like nothing more than a scheme to keep him out of circulation for a few hours. He was probably going to find out that somebody was doing it for his own good! Everybody was so damned solicitous of his good! The State Department once had airlifted him out of Berlin on the same pretext . . . Good God, not Chatterton's doing, this, surely!

The General began to explore the house. A place as well equipped as this might very well have a jeep or some such conveyance for mountain travel. After all, he was presumed sleeping. He was not expected to do much exploring. He got his tails and dress shirt out of the closet—a woman's closet. His things smelled delicious. Just let Mrs. Norris get a whiff of them. The dear woman, he would have been better off having spent the night in her company, and by this night's end he might very well be content to retire into it.

A peculiar thing happened then: all the lights in the

house—and a fair number of them had been left lighted—dimmed down to where the General thought they were going out. Then they came on again. Something around the place was demanding an extraordinary amount of electric power. But there was not the sound of any motor anywhere, furnace, heater, freezer.

The General decided to go down to the basement, and if he found nothing there, to go outdoors. It would take Virginia almost a half-hour to reach the city, if that's where she was going. She had been gone ten minutes. He pulled on the striped sweater again for warmth over his coat, and catching a glimpse of himself in the closet mirror, his cropped hair bristling, the formal tails dangling behind him, he thought he looked like the King of the Cats.

The General found nothing electrical in the basement except a washing machine. But the curious thing about it all was, he did not even find a fuse box or a meter.

He was distracted, however, finding a filing cabinet, one drawer of which was padlocked. He had not the slightest qualm in opening the unlocked drawers. All accounts of Leo Montaigne's travels, it seemed by cursory examination. He wished fervently that he had more time. The young man had been a great many places, and had met a great many people—every one of whom was referred to by initials. It would take remembering to put all those initials to people. The General guessed that in one notebook perhaps one hundred sets of initials appeared. Who could remember the names behind them? There was only one answer as he saw it: there must be a code for them. He was sure of it, noting that each page was hand-numbered. Why trouble numbering pages except for quick individual reference?

As for the contents, they read at first like women's gossip at some God-forsaken military outpost: a place where the strain of isolation told on men's nerves and women's characters. After reading a few pages more, the General recognized the locale—the United States Embassy, and soon the country, the Netherlands.

Then the General read: "I have my bond! I negotiated it this morning, and the price I blush to say. Oh, what a rogue am I, sans peasant's clothes. A. must wear me now like an albatross forever. Dear A. So brilliant a woman, and to have had but one indiscretion. But what responsibility now that I know. I must not sleep. I wonder if she is up to violence? Who is not, being desperate? It will be better that we go home soon, where it is more difficult to hire assassins."

Very clearly, then, General Jarvis pieced together his recollection of Holland in the early years after the war. Madam Jennings had been the American ambassador, until for reasons of health she asked to be recalled. He had not seen her then, but he remembered it now. And he had remembered earlier this night how supple and feminine she was not long before then. And he also remembered that, having recently been invited to join the presidential cabinet, her work in hospital rehabilitation over the past five years had been cited, accounting presumably for her years out of public service. A sort of penitential withdrawal?

One more thing the General remembered while he searched the basement for a stout instrument: at the Chatterton dinner tonight Elizabeth Jennings' defiant self-pride when he had surprised her gazing after young Montaigne. He cursed himself and his one-track mind: he had thought her enamoured of the young man herself. And yet, he suspected more people than himself might have that notion.

He found a small crowbar among the garden tools and without hesitation wrenched the padlock from the cabinet door. As he had anticipated, there was an entire notebook of initials and the names which matched them, only in his code. A. evidently was too familiar a person to need a code. He was reasonably certain A. was Elizabeth Jennings, but he would have liked to be dead certain. The drawer contained also notebooks of detail about what was going on in the world in the 1920's. From Aimee to Vanzetti, the General thought, "Yes, we have no bananas," but plenty of bathtub gin.

His mind quickened to that notion and to a couple of things of simultaneous association: the assault on electrical power, and the smell he had first apprehended, arriving outside the cabin with Virginia—fermented corn!

He hastily closed the cabinet door—or tried to. Some of the papers he had pulled out had not been properly put back. And trying to push the front folder down to the bottom of the drawer, he caught his thumbnails on an envelope fastened to the back of the drawer door. It was a neat, obscure hiding place really, which only his chance carelessness had discovered. The envelope was fastened in place by the screws that went through the metal to the drawer handle. The General tore the envelope free. Inside it were a half-dozen letters addressed to one of the most famous royal pretenders now living in modest exile with, the General was fairly sure, his wife and family. He opened one envelope and read only the salutation: "My dear," and the signature, "Elizabeth."

He cursed softly, having not even a pocket in which to put them except his trousers. Awkward. He decided to take them nonetheless. No one as honourable as himself might ever have the chance.

Friends in high places: that was what Chatterton had said of the scoundrel! And no doubt enemies in hell.

He turned off the light and, waiting a long moment to accustom his eyes to the darkness, he went out through the basement door. The cabin was on high ground, and there was no sign of a garage anywhere. He still had not found an electric meter, so he took that search as his line of departure. The moon was high still, and against the brightened sky he located the electric and the telephone wires. Curious, it was only the telephone service that came up the hill along the road. His own heartbeat accelerated as he started down the scrubby mountainside following the electric line. He was virtually certain there was an independent power plant. He paused now and then and held his breath to listen. An owl was all he heard at first, then the singing of a machine came to him, and finally, men's voices.

He was some seconds listening, trying to locate their direction, when it suddenly broke through to him that he was sitting on the roof of a cave. He could feel the vibration in the earth beneath him.

He did not know much about making moonshine except that it required terrific heat, to say nothing of nerve. It would seem to him an occupation of last resort these days, and of small return. But what did he know? He had heard that the stuff was still bootlegged in the mountains, and he was sure as hell in the mountains. The question was, could he ever get out of the mountains?

One thing certain—an associate with private hootchmakers was right in character with Montaigne.

The General went down on his hands and knees and crept to the edge of the roof. A road twisted down from there like a dirty string in the moonlight. A truck—canvas-covered, perhaps a couple of tons' capacity—was parked directly beneath him, its tail half into the garage, for light shone out around it. And that was where the men were also.

The General listened. Theirs was very nearly a foreign language, so strong was the hill country dialect—less than thirty miles from the capital of the U.S.A. Gradually he could make out words, none of which meant a damned thing to him. He began to calculate his chances of stealing the truck.

Then one of the men said, "How long now, Red?" The words were as "twangy" as a saw. But the General could understand them.

"Half-hour. I calculate we can turn her off and let her cool while we go down."

"Think I ought to start loading?"

"Time enough. Deal another hand or two."

"I can't afford to lose no more."

"Shucks, man, your credit's good for a couple hours."

"What if he ain't there?"

"He better be there. Cash on Wednesday."

"I don't trust that boy much, Red. He's too pretty."

"Don't have to trust him. It's me what knows where the dynamite is—and you know something? I just don't think he carries insurance on his little old cabin . . . I can't open, can you?"

"Yeah, I'll open since I'm playing with your money."

The General resolved that even at the risk of his life, when that truck went down the mountain he was going with it.

19

Mrs. Norris, waiting in the park, felt her bones to be as cold as a stone bench, and observing the benches, a line of them along the path in the moonlight, she was reminded of tombstones. It was a miserably lonely watch she kept; a clock somewhere off in the night struck two. Was there ever an Irishman born, she wondered, who had any notion of time? It was the greatest of follies to have left the house with him in the first place.

A very few minutes later she decided that she had had what long ago her mother called an elegant sufficiency. Still, there was a package put into the tree, and if the whole business weren't nonsense, something had to be done about it. There was but one thing in her power, she decided, and immediately set about working her hand behind the stone plate into the hollow. She soon brought out into the moonlight a small neat package carefully tied with string.

It was her business only if she made it so. Not even a restless bird stirred to interrupt the silence. Mrs. Norris took the package beneath the nearest streetlamp, and painstakingly untied the string. She had in her hand, when the package was opened, several small, tight rolls of microfilm.

Mrs. Norris could scarcely breathe for the palpitations of her heart. She sucked in the night air for dear life. Finally her heartbeat slowed to more nearly normal and her hand grew steadier. If someone did come for the package, what could she do? It was not really a matter of bravery or cowardice, but rather of wisdom. Merely to watch and report was not going to prevent these things from passing into the hands of some culprit.

She opened her purse. She was in truth beginning to feel a bit uneasy on Tom's behalf. He was very bold, and however serious he had pretended to be, he was taking this all too much as a lark. It was too bad a person could see best with hindsight. There was nothing in her purse except money and keys—and room.

She dropped the package of microfilms into it, but—for Tom's sake it might turn out—she wanted to leave a package in the tree that a messenger—a courier, did they call them?— could pick up and believe that he had the real thing. Alas, she had nothing to leave . . . except Tom's own poems which she suddenly remembered to be in the pocket of her dress.

Would he ever get them back, she wondered. Ah, but he knew them by heart surely, having offered to recite them to her. She would have to chance it.

And perhaps this way, she thought, getting out the small bundle of them and putting them into the tree, they would win him a fame a poet could hallow only as a patriot. She pulled the stone plate forward, and standing back to survey it an instant, she thought it did resemble a mouthful of teeth surrounded by the swollen lips of the tree's wound. Poor thing, to have its wound opened for such desecration. Looking back from a few feet away, Mrs. Norris could not tell the fatal tree from its neighbours.

Mrs. Norris hastened out of the park. On a mission such as hers, the borrowing of a child's bicycle was surely conscionable. She took careful notice that she would remember the house, since there was no one in the house likely to remember her. She also took care not to try to mount the vehicle until she was on an isolated part of the street, lest she collapse with a racket. She got her backside well situated, her purse on the handlebar, the front wheel heading down a slight hill, one foot on a pedal and, with the other, she pushed off from the curbstone with all her might. She might not be as agile herself as she was in her youth, but the bicycles they were making now were more so. She travelled with the wind. She was very shortly on and over the Key Bridge, having observed no life there at all. But having crossed the bridge, she discovered she must be in Georgetown by the architecture. In fact, she was on Thirty-fourth Street; she had but to go to Thirty-first, and follow it till she found herself home.

Home. It was the only place for her surely, until she decided on what branch of police to contact. Besides, the General himself should be home now, and he was the man to advise her.

Tom, the villain, had never murmured a word about how close they had come back to home. And yet it was not close enough. Her legs were beginning to ache. She pushed on. Two or three cars passed her: a queer sight she must be in her hat. What odds? Where were they accustomed to queerer sights than this meeting place of the world?

She was almost there, glimpsing the numbers at every block, and God help her, it was past time. She was beginning to suspect the presence of ghosties in her wake: she dared not look back, chiefly lest she lose her balance, but out of a certain dread as well. Her imagination, surely. Look what had happened to Tam O'Shanter. But he had been in the bottle. Mrs. Norris wished fervently that she had been. Or better, asleep and all this a dream, a nightmare. It would be worth a tumble to try and wake up.

But Mrs. Norris did not tumble. In fact, she scraped her leg on the bicycle chain, and did not wake up. Then at long last she came to the drive of her own house, and turning, threw herself off the bicycle. She saw then that she had indeed been followed. The black car which had pursued her from such a distance that she had not been certain it was there at all, quickly closed the gap. Mrs. Norris picked herself up, caught up her purse and ran for the steps. The car following her allowed a soft purr of its siren. Mrs. Norris gasped with relief. The police had followed her home! She turned with as much dignity as she could to welcome them.

Two men in plain clothes stepped from the car before it was fully stopped and came up, holding open in their hands what she afterwards realized was identification. She did not have a chance to say a word.

One of them gave his name and office, Federal Bureau of Investigation, and then said, "May I see your purse, madam?"

Mrs. Norris gave it over bravely.

He glimpsed its contents and said, "You are under arrest on suspicion of espionage."

20

Tom went up in the hotel elevator to Mrs. Joyce's suite with a very uneasy feeling in his stomach. The last thing he had expected was an invitation up—unless of course the boss was here. That would be something else again. But supposing the Frenchman had doubled back on him and was here himself now?

"Much traffic tonight?" Tom tried amiably with the brass-buttoned operator of the lift.

"Depends which way you're going," the elevator man said. Tom had reached his level anyway.

Mrs. Joyce did have company. She opened the door to Tom and directly introduced him by his trade: "Tom works for Congressman Jarvis, Senator. Tom, this is Senator Chisholm."

Tom crumpled his hat in his hands. A woman senator was almost too fearsome. She was long-faced and homely, and probably as knowing as Abe Lincoln's wife. There was a woman Tom would have been afraid of, to judge her by the picture given in a book he had read. But, sure, Lincoln himself was a little afraid of her.

It was the Senator that put the bit in Tom's mouth the moment he turned his head toward her. "Now, young man, what's this you've discovered about Dr. d'Inde?"

"Is that his name?" said Tom, "Dandy?"

The senator looked at Mrs. Joyce.

"I think we had better hear his whole story, Senator," Mrs. Joyce said. "It may be clearer in the long run."

The senator nodded, leaned back in the armchair and closed her eyes. By God, Tom thought, if it gave her such a pain to look at him, what would a mirror do to her?

"Sit down, Tom," Mrs. Joyce said, "and tell it in your own way."

"Well, Mrs. Norris and I were sitting in the kitchen. It must've been going on midnight, for I was reading the late paper to her, you know, where Senator Fagan was sweeping out the State Department after the party tonight?" Mrs. Joyce nodded. "Well, the doorbell rang and I was the one answered it. There standing in all his ribbons and glory was a little man as though he had just popped out of a bandbox. He had a great sash across his breast with all the gems of the Andes shining in it . . ." That, Tom noticed, had pried open the eyes of the senator. "Well, he told me his name, and I'm ashamed to say I forgot it and the country that he's ambassador from, but I know it's South America."

"Ambassador Cru?" said the senator.

"Aye, that's the man," Tom cried. "It's a name I knew I'd remember if I didn't forget."

The senator nodded ever so slightly at Mrs. Joyce.

"Well, to make a long story short, he asked me if I could stand second for the boss . . ."

Helene said, "Please, Tom, don't make a long story short. And don't make it complicated. Tell us exactly what happened. The exact words if you can."

"Aw, I can't do that," Tom said. "I'm a simple man, and he was as elegant as a Greek bishop. The best I could make out of it was that the Frenchman challenged the boss to a duel at dawn with pistols, and I was to stand by him. Well, I couldn't very well stand by him till I found him, could I? So Mrs. Norris and I went out to look . . ."

"Hold on, Tom," the senator said. "Where was the duel supposed to take place?"

"Under the Key Bridge on the Arlington side. And he left the Frenchman's card with his name sitting up on it."

"D'Inde?" said Helene.

"How do you spell that?"

Helene spelled it aloud.

Tom shook his head. "Oh, now, it's not a name like that. His first name—Leo, Leo the thirteenth."

The senator sat bolt upright. "Leo? Montaigne?"

Tom beamed on her. "Now you've got it, ma'am."

"Then maybe I can give it back to you," the senator said. "You've put one man's name on another man."

"All right, we saw what we saw, didn't we?" Tom blurted out.

"There you're dead right, son. Go on with your story."

"We just missed the boss, Mrs. Norris and me, when we got to the ballroom, but then we saw you coming out with the Frenchman, Mrs. Joyce, and we figured if we could keep him in sight, well, he wouldn't be shooting up Congressman Jarvis."

Helene raised her hand to slow him down. "This is the important part, now, Tom. The challenge business I suspect is somebody's play for publicity—and it was meant to involve General Jarvis, not Congressman Jarvis. Do you agree, Senator?"

"I do," she said.

Tom scratched his head. "However in the world would I have got something as mixed up as that? I suppose it was him taking for granted I worked for General Jarvis." Tom squared his shoulders. "I do look sort of military myself, don't I?"

"Very soldierly," Helene said.

"And of course it was seeing the Frenchman here in the afternoon that was preying on my mind."

"Young man," Senator Chisholm said sternly, "there are some pretty important matters preying on my mind right now. Will you get on with what happened?"

"Yes, ma'am," Tom said, and accounted then with as few diversions as possible for him, Mrs. Norris' and his pursuit of d'Inde.

"You're sure of the address?" the senator said.

"Well, I'm sure of the house," Tom said, "and Mrs. Norris'll be sure of the number. She's a very exacting woman."

"Where is she now, did you say?"

"Where I left her, I hope to God, in that little park in Arlington watching the tree he hid the package in. I promised to go back for her soon." Tom sighed deeply. "Ah, but sure, I made the same promise to my mother in Ireland five years ago."

"Well, Mrs. Joyce," Senator Chisholm said, "now what do you think? You know the man. Is he really an art curator?"

"Oh, I should think so," Helene said, "but that would not obviate his being something else also, would it?"

"A foreign agent?" said Tom.

"Something like that," Helene murmured.

"It would not. In fact it would better his entrée, as they say in polite circles," the senator said. "I wish to glory I could reach decisions in a hurry like this young man does, even if they were wrong ones. And I wish I had taken a look at the diagrams he was trying to get an opinion on. But as I said, I make it a practice to talk about those things with nobody on the outside. And I mean nobody. If certain other members of the Armed Services Committee would follow the same practice . . . ah, well. But never tell me that women talk more than men." She got up wearily and went to the window where she looked down on the street. "What time is it?"

"Ten minutes after two," Helene said.

"Oh, Lord," said Tom. "Mrs. Norris'll be stiff as a weathervane."

"If it wasn't so near morning," the senator said, "I'd call the FBI. I know one of the boys up there, but I don't know where his home is. I don't like to kick this affair out in the open till we know whether it's sense or nonsense."

"How would it be," Tom ventured, and his heartbeat quickened at his own boldness, "to call Senator Fagan?"

Senator Chisholm twisted her head around to look at him without moving the rest of her body. "That would be just fine, son," she said some thirty seconds later, while she looked back to the street.

Tom looked at Mrs. Joyce, who shook her head slightly, suggesting that they were not partial to his idea.

"Do you have a car, Tom?" the senator asked.

"I do, your honour, and at your service."

The senator turned back into the room and picked up her coat. "Let's all go and pick up your Mrs. Norris, shall we?"

21

As soon as word came to her that her husband had arrived, Madame Cru hastened back to her table. She did pause long enough to invite Jimmie to join them. Jimmie wanted very much to see Cru. However, he had observed Dolores, looking out most dolorously on the scene and he might never again have a chance like this. When he caught her eye, he lifted his glass and indicated that he would be pleased to have her join him. With all his consultations he was beginning to feel like Bernard Baruch.

She came at a leisurely pace—to pick up the compliments which, alas, were as hard to get out as bloom among thistles.

Jimmie stood up. "May I buy you a drink? I shall have to

fetch it myself, I'm afraid, with the gentlemen of the press taking over the bar."

"Thanks," she said in a voice she must have worked to flatten. "But Leo won't let me." Curiously, she seemed to have worked at flattening more than her voice: the 'twenties again, when women seemed to have tried for silhouettes like baseball bats.

"You're a minor, then?"

"Sort of."

Jimmie smiled. "You're sort of lots of things, aren't you?"

"Jack-of-all-trades, that's me," she said. "What do you do?"

"I work for the government," Jimmie said.

"You aren't a member, are you?"

"Of what?"

"The Club Sentimentale."

"No. Just a visitor."

"That's what I thought." She sat back and appraised him frankly. "You just don't look like the type."

"Is that a compliment?"

She shrugged. "I think so."

Jimmie leaned forward and said with gentle inquisitiveness: "If I were to tell you that I don't think you look like the type either, would you be complimented?"

Obviously, she was not. She became quite peevish about it. "What d'you expect? I can't learn everything in a day, can I? I'm trying."

Jimmie seemed to have touched something very tender. "I didn't say you weren't the type," he tried to amend. "I merely suggested that you didn't look it."

"You're too deep for me," she said. "Got a cigarette?"

While Jimmie shook one out of his package, she took a cigarette holder as long as a piccolo from her purse. He smiled watching her try to work the filter tip into the holder, biting her tongue in concentration. She was very young and very pretty, and he decided to risk one more impertinence: "Whose daughter are you, Dolores?"

"My mother's and father's," she said without hesitation.

"Touché," Jimmie said. "I thought I might know them."

"Ha-ha," she said, and it was more speech than laughter. "I thought you might, too. They're in Europe now, I stay with my aunt."

"I see," Jimmie said.

"But she's got her own life to live."

"Of course," Jimmie murmured.

"I think a woman should as long as she can, don't you?"

"I suppose."

"After all, that's what we got the vote for."

"Oh yes," Jimmie said. "I'd forgotten about that."

He lighted her cigarette for her when she finally had it squeezed into the holder.

"What's your name?"

"Jimmie."

"Do me a favour, Jimmie?"

"Gladly, if it's in my power."

"Tell Leo how wonderful you think I was tonight."

"I shall tell him," Jimmie said. "But I don't think he'd fire you if I didn't."

"You don't understand."

"Perhaps not."

"But you will tell him?"

"All right, Dolores, I'll tell him."

"It's very important—terribly."

"You're in love with him, aren't you?" Jimmie said.

She nodded.

The prospect of the end of this affair did not make Jimmie any happier. He was not especially taken with this child. But the contemplation of anyone young—or for that matter, of anyone decent—being in love with Leo Montaigne troubled him.

"Why does he call this place the Club Sentimentale?" Jimmie changed the subject painlessly.

"He says it's truth spelled backwards."

Which confirmed for Jimmie his suspicion that Montaigne was above all a cynic.

"Who are all those men?" she asked, for at that moment the members of the press began to spill into the room. "Are they all reporters?"

"Well, I don't know about all of them, but some of them are. They seem to have come in with Ambassador Cru."

"Oh, that's for the duel!"

"Do you think there will be one, Dolores?"

She shrugged. "Leo says so."

"Because the General is supposed to have carried off Leo's girlfriend?" She nodded. "But I thought you and Leo were in love."

"I'm in love with Leo, but he's in love with Virginia. Or that's what everybody thinks."

"I should have learned a long time ago," Jimmie said, "not to give advice where it's not asked of me. But at the risk of your telling me to go to the devil, Dolores, I want to suggest that Leo is not in love with any human being—only with a peculiar set of dream characters that he thinks he has created himself."

She looked at him and smiled, as though she herself was enchanted now by him. "That sounds so pretty," she said. "You talk just like Leo does sometimes."

Which, Jimmie supposed, was why such a world as "The Sentimentale" could exist at all. "I must now be about my father's business," he said, and realized what he had para-phrased. "Heaven help me," he added.

The reporters had discovered Maria Candido. For the first time now the night promised them some game worth the candle. They were coaxing one little song out of her when Jimmie went out to the bar to find Ambassador Cru.

Behind him he could hear Maria's warm-up trill, and the beginning of a bawd's tale:

"There was a fair maiden
"Who with brains wasn't o'erladen
"But laden she was just the same . . ."

"Everybody! Sing, 'tra-la-la, tra-la-la' . . ."

"Excellency," Jimmie said at the bar, "may I introduce myself? I'm James Jarvis. I understand you have been with my father."

"You are misinformed. I have merely delivered a challenge, acting on behalf of my friend, Leo Montaigne."

"May I ask who acted on behalf of my father?"

"His secretary, his confidential friend and his servant."

"Ah," said Jimmie, "that one! Tell me, excellency, if the message reached him, would you really expect my father to answer such a challenge?"

"Are you accusing me, sir, of acting in bad faith?"

"Perhaps I am, if you have gathered all these reporters without having ascertained that the message ever did reach him."

The small bandbox diplomat brought himself to attention. "You, sir, have impugned my honour . . ."

Jimmie interrupted him. "Save it; your honour, I mean, and your breath. I think it must have been pretty well arranged that my father would not show up. What's it all about, Excellency—a smoke screen? There was another challenge thrown down tonight—a little more important to Americans. Where's Montaigne?"

Jimmie crashed his fist on the bar and made the glasses bounce.

"You, sir, are a greater boor than your father," the ambassador said, and turned his back.

The blonde hostess was pouring out straight gins as far as he could judge. It turned his stomach to watch her go round to each glass then with a spoonful of something pink.

"Castor oil was never like that," Jimmie said, beginning to enjoy the boisterousness of his act. He suspected he could tumble this card house . . . but not too soon. "Where's your boss, honey?"

The blonde threw him a venomous look. "He just stepped outdoors. And I dare you to do the same thing . . . Mr. James."

"I just might," Jimmie said. "I could stand some fresh air."

Maria was really warmed up in the back room, so were the boys around her. The whole place had begun to sound like the *Hot Mikado*.

22

Mrs. Norris went quietly, as they say. After all, if ever a lady had an alibi, she assumed she had one. Never before this morning had she been in Washington at all.

Even as she told her story in the investigation room, however, she realized that it was going to require corroboration. The skepticism with which the agents viewed her account of the beginning of the chase was very discouraging.

A duel? In this day and age?

Over what?

Mrs. Norris closed her mouth on that subject permanently. It did not become Mr. James in any way, strangely, in that instant Mrs. Norris first felt the sting of truth.

When she looked at it from all directions she was in quite

a predicament. One of the men was running the microfilm through a machine. He shut it off then and turned to her. "I don't suppose you know what this film is about at all, do you, ma'am?"

"I've told you exactly what I know about it," Mrs. Norris said. "I'd never have touched the little package myself if I wasn't afraid it would fall into evil hands. But I could not stand in the cold all night waiting for an Irishman."

"My name is Mulrooney," one of the investigators said.

"More's the pity you have to hear the truth then," Mrs. Norris said, and the other man gave vent to a smile. One of them was human, at least.

"Would you like a lawyer, ma'am?"

"Will my word mean any more to you if you get it through the mouth of a lawyer?"

Mr. Mulrooney said, "We were thinking of your interests. We'll take care of ours, I think."

"Your constitutional rights," the other one added.

"If I was to take you to the house where I saw this man— this Frenchman. According to the Irishman, he's French, that is. He'll probably turn out a Hindu. If I were to take you there and show you the baluster where he had the package hidden, would you believe me?"

"My dear woman," Mulrooney said, "do you suppose we picked up your trail out of thin air?"

"Oh," Mrs. Norris said, and after a moment, "Then you have the Irishman, too?"

Neither man answered her. They were not likely to tell her

if they had, of course, but it made her feel a little more tender about Tom Hennessy. But it all meant that they were themselves on the trail of the Frenchman before she and Tom ever put their feet into it. And this made her wonder if Mrs. Joyce was in any way implicated. It all came much too close to Mr. James, whose innocence in any issue she would proclaim from a burning stake if need be.

"Now, let's hear the story again," Mulrooney said. "Just what did you intend to do with the package? Who was your contact? When's your next rendezvous?"

"My only rendezvous of the night was with Tom Hennessy, and if ever I keep another in my life, it won't be with him."

"And what were you going to do with the package?"

"I was going to consult my lawyer on it."

"Congressman Jarvis?"

Mrs. Norris clamped her lips tightly over her teeth.

"You know, ma'am, the Federal Bureau of Investigation is the proper channel for such information. We are very willing to cooperate with Congress, but we are better trained in investigation than most congressmen."

"Congressman Jarvis was once the district attorney of New York. So I daresay he could investigate along with the best of you."

"For God's sake, let's go out for coffee and let her think it over," Mulrooney said to his partner, and wiped his hands and his forehead with his handkerchief.

"I could do with a cup of tea myself while I'm waiting," Mrs. Norris said, "if you can arrange it, please."

23

"It's a good thing for my plumbing," Senator Chisholm said at the top of her voice, "that I spent a good part of my young days on a tractor."

"She gets us there," Tom said, and gave the steering wheel an affectionate pat. "Doesn't she, Mrs. Joyce?"

"But where?" said Helene. "That's the question."

"Right here," Tom said, and drove up to the park gate and turned off the motor. He stuck his head out the car window and whistled the first few bars of *Annie Laurie*. He did not get even an echo in response. With the next passage he woke a couple of robins from their sleep. They gave him two chirps apiece.

"We'd better get out and look," the senator said.

"If anything's happened to the dear woman," said Tom, "she'll never forgive me. Neither will the boss."

They walked, the three of them, into the park which was very still and full of shadows in the moonlight. A shiver of wind moved among the leaves.

"Hadn't I better have a look in the tree?" said Tom when it was obvious that no mortal other than themselves was about.

The two women nodded.

Watching him slide his hand in behind the stone plate, Senator Chisholm murmured, "Wouldn't Fagan like to be in my shoes right now? And wouldn't I be glad to loan them?"

Tom returned, empty-handed. "I can't find a thing, and the poor woman's gone. Do you suppose she's been done in? A fine woman like that 'ud be a great loss to the world."

"Don't set up the wake just yet," the senator said. "She may be as wily as yourself and just as much alive."

"That'd be the best thing that could happen to both of us," Tom said fervently. "She may even be off on more of an adventure than we are. Sure, I'd have been here myself taking this chance instead of her if she could've driven the car."

"Where's the house with the woman and all the children?" the senator asked. "You'd better drive us there, Tom. If we're this far into it, we had better go far enough to find out what it's all about."

"My very thought, ma'am," Tom said, and skipped ahead of them to open the car door.

"Did you know he had a family, Mrs. Joyce?" the senator asked when they were in the car again.

Tom wished he could muffle Sophie, the better to hear himself.

"I've known him only professionally—and not so long at that," Helene said. "He's been very helpful to me in my efforts to get the sculpture commission I told you about. He knows all the tastes and disposition of this town."

"So it would seem," the senator said. "He'd be all the more useful for that, wouldn't he?"

It seemed like a ruminative question so no one answered. In fact, no one spoke at all as they drove across the bridge and back into Washington proper. Tom craned his neck as they crossed the river, but not a stir of activity seemed to be moving there on either bank, no more than if the dawn was never expected. Tom parked the car in front of the house not far from Dupont Circle.

"You'd better come with us, young man," the senator said, "since you're the one who was here before."

It never occurred to Tom that she might wish to exclude him. But that was a woman's way: when things got interesting, they expected a man to stand back and let them push up ahead to where everything was happening. On the way up to the darkened house, and while his finger was on the doorbell where there was no name plate, Tom brooded over it.

No buzzer sounded, but presently a woman came out to the glass door in the vestibule and pulled aside the curtain.

"Well, Tom?" the senator said shortly.

"That's her."

She opened the door to them, seeing, no doubt, that it

was the women who held the balance of power. "What is it you want?"

"I'm Senator Grace Chisholm, madam, and I'd like to speak to your husband. If he's not here, then I'd like to speak to you."

"He's not here. Let me see your identification."

The senator opened her purse and brought out a wallet Tom thought better suited to an industrialist.

"I guess I'd know you from your picture anyway, Senator. What time is it?" Even as she asked, she allowed them to follow her into the house.

Helene looked at her watch. "Twenty minutes to three."

"George won't be home tonight," she said.

Helene laid her hand on the senator's arm to draw her attention, and then shook her head.

Tom had forgotten what it was, but he was pretty sure Dandy's name wasn't George. Both women cast him a look of inquiry. He shrugged. What could he tell them? He was sure this was the place—the nameplate missing from the box, the balusters in front of the house. And sure, he had recognized the woman.

It was a dull, middle-class living room she led them into, with gaudy reproductions on the wall. A glassed-in bookcase held a few paper-backed books, not all American. There were toys strewn about, and some of elegance above any child's reach.

"Will he go directly to work, Mrs. d'Inde?" Helene ventured.

The woman turned on her. "What did you call me?"

"Mrs. d'Inde," Helene repeated, having cast the die. She edged toward a table on which there was a wedding photograph.

"That's not my name," the woman said. "What do you people want at this hour and where's your search warrant?"

Helene by then had picked up the photograph. The man was doubtless Henri d'Inde, though much younger than he was today. "Do you ever go to the National Museum?" she asked the woman. And when she got no answer, she said, "I know him from there, you see, as Henri d'Inde."

"So you're the one," the woman said. "I knew he had another one somewhere lately. Shameless . . ."

Senator Chisholm interrupted. "Madam, you misunderstand! Mrs. Joyce is an artist. Your husband is interested in . . ." The senator faltered.

"We think your husband is a spy," Tom blurted out, taking over. He could not do any worse than the experts, he thought, and the truth to a woman betrayed about anything that did not concern her betrayal was, he reasoned, welcome. "We're not here to talk to you about his morals." Tom meanwhile had looked about the room. It was the toys in high places that most interested him, toys that showed no signs of having been at the battering mercy of children. Tom reached up and touched one of them—a bottle with no bottom. He had wondered how a man came home in a dress suit to a house like this without a working-man's explanation. "Your husband's a magician, isn't he?"

"So?"

Tom was conscious of the mute admiration of his two companions. In fact, he was rather in awe of himself. "So where was he supposed to be playing tonight?"

"At some private club," she said. "I don't ask that as long as he brings home the money afterwards."

"Will you take the word of a United States senator that he attended the Beaux Arts Ball tonight?" Senator Chisholm put in.

"If this is your husband," Helene added, pointing to the picture.

"Furthermore," said the senator, "I sat at the same table with him at dinner."

"You, too?" the poor woman cried out.

"Well," said Tom, "the man *is* a magician." No one seemed to appreciate what he thought was humour. He strode across the room to the library table then, on the shelf of which he had spied an album. There was scarcely a performer in the world who didn't keep one. "You don't mind if I look at this?" he said, already at it. "The Great d'Artagnan," he read aloud.

"What's the name?" the senator said.

Tom repeated it by syllables, but Mrs. Joyce pronounced it this time.

"It's a wonder things couldn't be spelt," Tom said, "to match the sound they make."

"You're Mrs. d'Artagnan, then?" the senator said.

"I am."

"How long have you been married?"

"Six years and twins."

"Seven children," Helene said, understanding her immediately.

"Does he talk about them?" the woman said rather wistfully.

"Quite often," Helene said, "and of you." The latter she added out of kindness.

"Are you sure it's me?" the woman said. She turned to Tom. "What's all this about him being a spy?"

"I think that's a matter better gone into in daylight," the senator interrupted, "and better with the great d'Artagnan himself. Don't you think so, Tom?"

It was to muzzle him she consulted him, Tom knew, seeing the glare in the old eagle's eye. "Sure it was only a manner of speaking in the first place, ma'am," he said. "The truth is we're looking for him to find out what he knows of the whereabouts of a friend of mine."

"A lady-friend?"

"Aye," Tom said, for whatever else she was, Mrs. Norris was a lady. "He went out of here with a suitcase. Now, do you know where he was spending the night?"

"All there was in the suitcase, I can tell you, was his card tricks," the woman said. "I packed them for him myself." This Tom knew to be the truth, that she had packed the suitcase for him. "He often sleeps right in the car if he's going to be late," she went on, "or that's where he tells me he's sleeping."

"It's a good place," Tom murmured.

"Anyway, he was going to some private club he said to make a few extra dollars."

"You had a few words on the matter, you and him, didn't you?" Tom said.

"It's you are the spy, it seems to me, spying on us," the woman said.

"Well," Tom said, aggrieved, "I had my reasons."

"All right," the poor wife said, "if he was meeting your friend there, I'll tell you where he said he was going—the Club Sentimentale. Do you think he was telling the truth?"

"He just might," said Tom, "for I've heard the name of the place before tonight."

Outdoors, Helene said, "D'Artagnan and the three Mus-keteers."

"That's us!" said Tom. "Ach, the poor woman."

"I don't think she's altogether without resources," the sen-ator said.

"She isn't without kids, sure," said Tom, "if you can call them resources."

The senator laughed for the first time at something he had said that night. Too late, m'lady, he thought. You'll not win me now by humouring my humour.

"Take us back to the hotel, Tom," the senator said. "The best thing to do is to put this all in the hands of the FBI right now."

It might seem best to her, Tom thought, driving back. But for himself and since he had contributed no small share to the unravelment he felt entitled to an opinion—he had another idea.

He stayed in the lobby when they went upstairs. He

changed his dollar and a half into dimes and went into a phone booth. Having spent part of the night in the company of one senator, he had the courage to try to reach another— one more to his liking, a man, and a man willing and ready to tackle a case like this. Tom started by calling Senator Fagan's favourite columnist at the Washington *Herald*. It was a bold start, and a good one.

24

They were taking their damn good time starting to load the booze, the General thought, especially for a pair waiting to collect on it. At best he had a delicate bit of athletics before him, for he could not hoist himself into the truck before they had loaded it, and he was not as nimble of leg as he was ambitious. He could hear the shuffle of playing cards, the squirt (he supposed) of tobacco juice slicing the air and occasionally nicking the hot stove.

The thing he feared most was that Virginia might return and find him missing before he really was missing, and that he might be searched for here. After all, this should be a well-kept secret until the proper moment, especially if it were stoked with dynamite. A touch-and-go business, to say the least.

He decided on total calculation, however, to risk a return to the house. There was something there he wanted, and his joints needed loosening. Up the hill again he scrambled like an infantry private on night manoeuvres. Dust man was and to dust returneth. The General spat a mouthful of it into the face of the stars.

He went in through the basement and up the stairs where he made a great bulging heap of pillows beneath the blanket: a shape he hoped resembled Ransom Jarvis. The prone sight of him could forestall an early search, he hoped. But it was a revolting lump to contemplate. Given time, he might have stuck pins in it himself.

He was standing back to further scrutinize his work when the electric lights took a turn for the brighter. That meant they had turned off the power on the still below, he reasoned, and would soon be ready to go.

The General hastened to the mantel, intending to lift one of the pistols just in case the boys needed persuasion some-where along the way. But when he got to the wall, the racks were bare.

Both pistols, it would seem, had gone down the mountain with Virginia.

"All the king's horses," he murmured to himself, march-ing down the basement steps, and down the hill again, "all the king's horses and all the king's horses' asses."

The boys were loading up. He could hear the rattle of bottles as they humped cases of them onto the truck. Did they have labels, he wondered . . . Old Dynamite, maybe. He could tell from the next pattern of sound that they were roping the cases into place, and for that he was grateful. If they had to rope, there was room in the truck for him.

He fell to speculating on how long it would take the stuff they were making tonight to ripen and mellow. They could take their time with a setup like this, and maybe turn out a tolerable keg. There were, no doubt, some fine old family formulae in the hill country around Washington, coming all the way down from the times of the Whisky Rebellion.

One of the men came out in the open then and got into the truck. The General made ready to jump. But the other fellow was not yet in sight. It trembled his nerves, but the old soldier held steady.

The driver moved the truck out of the garage and the General thought for one bad instant that he was left behind, for he could no longer leap off to the top of the truck. He got a whiff of coffee on the wind then, and the driver got out of the truck and went into the cave again. The General eased himself down beyond sight of the door and, catching hold of a scrub pine, swung himself over and dropped to the ground with the quiet alacrity that would have done credit to a guerrilla scout. He climbed over the truck gate and lay down flat between where the cases were roped into place and the tailgate.

There was room for two like him, he thought, in the truck though not, perhaps, in the world.

25

Jimmie suspected from the blonde's attitude that once he stepped outdoors, he might have to wrestle her to get in again, and while nothing about the place now suggested that anyone in it was expected to behave like a gentleman . . . Besides, she was bigger than he was.

Before going out, however, he made one more attempt to reach home by telephone; quite futile. He got his own hat and then took fifty cents and laid it, not too gently, in the saucer.

"Thanks," the blonde called out as though genuinely surprised.

Jimmie stepped into the night and closed the door between him and the raucous soprano. The hack stand was empty except for a car bearing a PRESS sign. Wherever Montaigne had gone, he was not anywhere in sight.

The Arlington side of the Potomac under the Key Bridge. Jimmie got into his car and turned it up to the highway. It wasn't far. Francis Scott Key. Oh, say, can you see by the dawn's early light? He wondered if, by any chance, Mrs. Norris was huddled beneath it, trying to keep herself warm. Not a car on the road. Suddenly then, two small round bores of light: a car, Jimmie realized, coming at enormous speed. He pulled over to the side, himself slowed down almost to a stop. He did stop suddenly, and stepped out of his car almost simultaneously with the other car's passing of him: it was as fast as reflex for he recognized the Jaguar as soon as it was a few yards from him, and he got out of his car shouting, trying to wave it down. But it sped on through the night like an earthbound comet, streaking out smoke like a tail.

It was a quiet and reverent oath Jimmie swore while he got back into his car. Whatever his father's follies, he would not drive like that under any circumstance Jimmie could imagine.

He was, for the first time, truly alarmed. There was no point turning in the Jaguar's wake. Unless it crashed up, he could not catch it. He drove on and across the Key Bridge, and then parked in the circle. He took the flashlight from the glove compartment, perhaps as a weapon, for he moved as surely, and as tremblingly, as though some fate had taken hold and now directed him.

At the end of the bridge where the grass sloped down from the roadside to the river's edge, he stood and flashed his light first upon the ground at his feet. It had the softness of spring, and there was indeed a great circular indentation as of a car swung hard and fast to the beginning of the incline. The tyre's size was that of a Jaguar.

Jimmie peered down then toward the river's edge. He half-expected what waited discovery there, the dark, huddled shape of a man where he had been tumbled down the slope. Jimmie, trained as he was in matters of evidence, avoided the direct way down lest he spoil certain markings. Thus he went down the embankment a few yards to the north and approached the body from along the river bank.

He touched nothing, but shone his light in the face of Leo Montaigne. He felt for the pulse. There was none, though the flesh was warm. Jimmie saw the area of the wound, and leaning a little closer, could smell the powder. He had been shot at very close range, and he had doubtless died instantly.

26

Jimmie did not expect to find the Jaguar at the Club Sentimentale, but he knew that among the things he would find
there, and as quickly as anywhere else, was a telephone with
which to call the police. It had to be done even though it add
confoundment to confusion. Jimmie had several thoughts
about Montaigne; any number of people might have killed
him and probably with good reason. But not very many
people could have made it look like General Jarvis' doing. It
was sheer chance he had seen the car himself, and could so
accurately call the time of the murder.

Jimmie went into the club as though he intended to butt
his way if anyone obstructed him.

But the blonde called out to him from the bar, "Leo ain't back yet, honey."

"I know," Jimmie said, "I've just seen him. What time did he go out that door?"

"Three a.m.," the blonde said. "I know because it's closing time. Not tonight though. We're staying here till dawn."

Jimmie looked at his watch. Montaigne had been murdered between three and three-ten.

A reporter was in the phone booth, for which Jimmie was grateful. Why the hell had he been raised with a conscience like a deacon's and a mismatched father? He pushed through the raucous room where Candido had been hoisted up on a table, the better to lead the riot. It was a crazy, mad cabaret jumping on the banks of the Potomac. Jimmie flailed his way through to where some of the boys had taken up with Dolores. They were trying to get a rival songfest going with the popular songs of the day.

Jimmie simply caught the girl by the arm and dragged her away from them toward the back room. "I've got to talk to you about Leo," he said.

It was enough. She went willingly.

The back room was a combination storeroom for bar supplies and dressing room. He set the girl down at a dressing table and pulled up a chair.

"Dolores, I've got to have some information. It's very important, and you'll know why pretty soon. What do you know about this Virginia Allan?"

The girl shrugged. "There's all kinds of stories about her. Somebody said she used to be with Texas Guinan, whoever she was. I heard she wrote novels once, you know, a writer with three names?"

Jimmie nodded. "What did Leo tell you about her?"

"Nothing. Except he owed a lot to her. He always wanted me to imitate her. Then he said when I got to be just like her . . . it would be all right."

She had changed her mind on what to say at the end of that sentence, Jimmie knew. "Was tonight your first big chance?"

She nodded that it was.

"How did he like it?" Jimmie was remembering her asking that he tell Leo how good she was.

"He said it was just fine, but not yet."

"Not yet what?"

"I couldn't go on yet, I guess."

"Did he promise to marry you, Dolores?"

Her eyes were wide and very surprised that he should know.

"When you got to be just like Virginia Allan, Leo was going to marry you, wasn't he?"

She countered with a question: "Where's Leo?"

Jimmie kept hammering with his own questions. "Where does Virginia live?"

"I don't know."

"Ah, but you do, Dolores. You know everything about her that Leo knew."

The girl looked up at him. "Is she dead?"

Jimmie hated to hurt her, but life would have been much more cruel to this child if Leo Montaigne had lived. "No, Dolores, but Leo has been killed, and I suspect she may be implicated." He said it very quietly and laid his hand on hers.

Dolores seemed to wither, her mouth quivering, and then the tears ran full in her eyes.

"The best thing now is if you can help me find her," Jimmie said.

"Where's Leo?" she asked.

"There's nothing you can do for him," Jimmie said firmly. "He'll be taken care of. But there will be a great deal of trouble, I assure you, and I will try to take care of you."

She dried her eyes and nodded her understanding of her need for it. The very young, he thought, were the least equipped to show false concern over others when it was themselves they most cared to protect.

"Where is the most likely place to find her?" Jimmie persisted. "Especially if she has a man with her, where would she be likely to take him?"

"I guess maybe to Leo's cabin." Then she thought about that. "But Leo hasn't been gone that long, Mr. Jarvis. It takes almost a half-hour to get there."

Jimmie got up. "Put your coat on, Dolores. You know where it is?"

"I think so. He . . . he took me there once."

"I understand," Jimmie said. "Get your coat." He looked around and saw a hallstand on which a light grey coat was hanging . . . so much the schoolgirl's coat. "Is this it?"

She nodded.

Jimmie held it for her. "However did you meet up with him at all, child?"

"I'm not a child. I told you, my aunt. Or didn't I? Anyway, she's—or she *was*—in love with him. Lots of women are. Were."

Jimmie took her out to the car by the side door, and then because he was afraid she might run away if he left her, he decided not to go back to telephone. It was a dilemma he had not anticipated, and his conscience, for the time being, was just going to have to be stuck with it.

Dolores steered him through the town and out of it with an expert's eye. He was put in mind of the accuracy of his own youth when it came to directions. But it was like pointing out the marvels of a baby who could remember where his toys were, or recognize his own family. What the devil else did he have to think about?

Jimmie himself suddenly had quite something else to think about. The car had no more than eased up the first foot-hill when Dolores eased her little thighs along the distance between them, and put her little hand under his arm and her little head upon his shoulder.

"Are you married, Mr. Jarvis?"

Which made him laugh: not the question, but the formality of "Mr. Jarvis."

"No."

"I didn't think you were. You're so, so debonair. I just love older men. I guess I'm addicted to them."

"Are you?"

"Is that the wrong word?"

"I don't know. It's you that suffers from the affliction."

"I do suffer," she said. "You're so understanding."

"Just how old are you, Dolores?"

"Fifteen."

He gave her a ruthless nudge with his elbow. "Then get the very devil over in that corner and think about Leo," he said. "You're old enough for that."

He had just driven a minor across the state border, and she hanging onto him like a Virginia creeper.

27

Once the truck took off down the mountain, its canvas slapping like sails in the wind, the General felt fine. In fact, he had never felt better in his life. An old bear was not to be caught in a mousetrap. He put his hand in his pocket and touched the letters belonging to a cabinet member, letters, the very contents of which, although he could but surmise them, set the blood of an old warrior coursing. He was a knight without armour.

Oh, by God, he had his work set out for him, for he was resolved to put everything in order, everyone anxious at ease: such was the elixir he had got with this new sense of his own power. What power was like that of a righteous man who has escaped dishonour and with the weapons at hand with which to destroy a cad! Blackmailer! Bootlegger! Bloodsucker!

Oh, Montaigne, you fraud, you maggot, you fly in the champagne of life!

A thunderous rattle broke in upon the General's reverie. It was a moment before he realized they had crossed over the wooden bridge and onto the highway. He sat up on one elbow and peered out a crack in the canvas: it was beautiful country, this, but he would certainly hate to have traversed it in a litter. He was thinking again of the Civil War and—since he was on his back—of its wounded. The hills might well be haunted, the issues not yet at rest.

By the glory of the skies, it was a night for poetry as well as justice! A night? A morning. For yonder cracked something brighter than moonlight haloing the mountaintops.

Then the General heard a sound almost beloved, so that it made him sad. He watched and waited and saw his dear Jaguar go roaring up the road, away from him and out of sight. He touched his lips with two fingers and blew the kiss into the night. Then he lay back and cushioned his head in his locked fingers. He would be a long time buying another Jag on a pension. It was altogether too melancholy a thought. Better to plan the morning's triumph.

28

Tom had not dreamed of talking to Senator Fagan himself. Well, he had dreamed of it, but the best he expected to happen to him awake was that he would get through to a secretary's secretary. He probably did, getting through to quite a number of people, none of whom was more than half-awake, and none of whom more than half-believed him. But no one would chance dismissing him entirely, not with that story.

What he needed for this sort of operation, Tom thought, dredging his fourteenth dime out of his pocket, was a government subsidy. He put the thought out of his mind immediately as unpatriotic.

On all his calls, Tom had started by saying that he had seen a man behaving very much like a spy depositing secret documents and that the woman he had set to watch had disappeared. But by the time he got into the explanation of the Frenchman with two lives, one of which he lived under the name of d'Artagnan—a name never meant for an Irish tongue—most of his listeners were prepared to consign their share in the fame of exposure to someone else in the Senator's chain of command.

But on the fourteenth dime, as soon as he got an answer, Tom took hold of the phone by the mouthpiece. "Now listen to me, whoever you are at the other end there. I've had enough nonsense. Are you awake?"

There was ever so brief a pause, then came a resonant: "It's milking time, isn't it?"

Something in that voice reached Tom in his every fibre. It prompted him to give more what he thought was wanted than what he thought he had. "I think I've got onto a spy case, sir," he said very slowly and distinctly, "and the way I got onto it, I was trying, all innocent, aye, ignorant you might say, to find a certain Army general."

Tom waited, scarcely able to hear anything above the throb of his own heartbeat. Nonetheless, he caught the sucking sound of shock and pained indignation. Then that voice said, "What army?"

The question stunned him. He assumed it was the American. He had never thought to ask. Of course, it was the American. "American, sir."

"How many stars?"

"Beg pardon, sir?"

179

"How many stars does the General have?"

"I don't rightly know, sir, but I'm sure as many as he could get. He's that sort."

"What prompted you to call Senator Fagan at this hour of the morning?"

Could he be wrong, Tom wondered, about who was at the other end of the phone? "Sure, sir, it all just happened."

"Are there any documents involved?"

"There are, sir. That's what I called about. I saw him hiding them in a tree like a squirrel its nuts."

"Well, God bless you, man! You stay right where you are until one of my boys comes and gets you. Let me have the address."

Tom gave the address and then thanks to heaven, for his dime's worth of telephone had just run out. He went out of the booth and got the night clerk to sell him a cigar for his last dime, a very particular cigar for a very particular gentleman.

"Do you want it gift-wrapped?" the clerk said, and yawned in his face.

29

Senator Chisholm was surprised to learn that her friend, Luke Forsman, an investigator for the Federal Bureau of Investigation, was in the office.

"It's that kind of night," he explained on the phone.

"It sure is," the senator said earnestly. "You don't happen to be working on the Chatterton dinner party?"

"Don't I?" Forsman said wearily.

"Then why hasn't somebody been in touch with me? I was there, too, you know."

"Have you been home since, Senator?"

"No, come to think of it, I haven't."

"I'm going to tell you, it's asking a lot of the FBI to know where people are when they don't know themselves. Do you want to give us a deposition, Senator? Some other people there want to. Matter of fact, most everybody in Washington wants to."

"Including an art curator called d'Inde?"

"We'll get to him," Forsman said.

"I think you're going to have to. I doubt he's going to come to you. Have you got an alias 'd'Artagnan' on him? Did you know he's a magician by night as well as an art man by day?"

"I'd have to have a subpoena before answering all those questions for you, Senator. Or is this part of the deposition you want to give us?"

"See here, Luke. Sometime tomorrow morning—this morning—I'm going to get caught in Fagan's dragnet because I was at that dinner. I don't think it's accidental that it happened to me, but I can't prove that. Just the same, I don't want to be one of the poor fishes he throws back into public life to sink or swim. I've had twenty years in the government and I'm good for a few more."

The young man listening to her sighed very gently, but not quite soundlessly. "I have a suggestion, Senator. As long as you're still up and around, why don't you go back to the Chatterton house? You might talk to your hostess."

"Has she talked to you?"

"Right now she'll talk to anyone, and maybe you'll understand what we're up against when you hear her. Everybody wants to have a dawn clearance on this damn business, but they won't stop filibustering."

"Easy, Luke."

"Sorry, Senator. Go along there. It'll be easier for us if you're all in one place."

"All right, but I'm going to bring a young man with me I think you ought to talk to."

"Sure . . ." Then he asked abruptly, "Senator, is he Irish?"

"As sure as the Pope's a Catholic."

"Where did you find him?"

"That's what I called you about, Luke, but you wanted it under oath."

"I'd better have it now," Forsman said, "oathed or un-oathed."

Senator Chisholm told him briefly of Tom and of the visit to the house of d'Artagnan the magician.

"You're right," Forsman said. "Bring him with you. I'll want to talk to him."

"What about Mrs. Joyce?"

"I suppose she'd better come too, if she's a witness."

When the senator hung up the phone she said, "I think we have a young man, don't we?"

Helene looked down to the street from the window. "His car is there. I doubt he'd go any place without it."

When they reached the lobby, however, the night clerk handed Helene the key to the jalopy and told them of Tom's phone calls, the purchase of the cigar, and of his departure. "He said you could use the car, Mrs. Joyce."

"That was optimistic of him," Helene said. "Shall we take it, Senator?"

"It's not a question of shall, girl, it's a question of can. Can we take it? Come on."

"Where would you say Tom went?" Helene opened the car door for the older woman.

"Well, I won't say he went over to the enemy. Let's just say he decided on a different commander."

30

Mrs. Norris was just finishing her cup of tea when another investigator joined the two who had been interrogating her. He was introduced as Mr. Forsman.

"Well, this looks pleasant enough," he said, "tea. I didn't know we had such facilities."

"We don't," Mulrooney said.

"Ah. It can't be said we persecuted you anyway, Mrs. Norris."

"I am not saying a thing. I have lived a life of respectability, and I do not take easily to the notion of being under arrest."

"There are such things, you know, as protective custody," Forsman said, arching his eyebrows slightly, as though he hoped she would cotton to the notion.

"Are you telling me they plucked me up in my own back yard and hied me here for that? I do not believe it, sir."

Forsman sighed. "And there are such things, I believe, as honest mistakes."

"Ah, now, you're talking, man. I knew the moment I got the tea there was something up."

Forsman grinned ever so slightly. "Hold on now, Mrs. Norris, I was rather thinking it was you who had made the honest mistake. If we've made one, it will take us a great deal longer to find it out—and longer still to admit it. I know this is going to upset you, but I assure you I have enough work to do tonight not to ask it if I didn't need it—I want you to go over your story again, for me this time. I've just picked up a little information I'd like to try and fit into it."

Mrs. Norris ruffled her shoulders, but she started at the beginning, relating her adventure with Tom.

Now and then Forsman checked some notes he had in his hand and nodded, she presumed at some verification of her story.

"Now, this French fellow," Forsman said when she was finished, "would you say he acted as though he felt at home?"

"Except with the baby, but to tell the truth, I didn't hold that against him, for not many men can take over when the wee one is skirling like that."

Forsman nodded.

"Oh, something I forgot to mention—he stepped out into the vestibule once, as though he was going to the mail box," Mrs. Norris said. "But it was Tom's notion that he took the nameplate off the door, for it was missing a few seconds later when Tom went in to look."

"Is Tom a reliable sort?"

"You're asking the wrong person for that opinion," Mrs. Norris said, "but he must have something steady to recommend him. He's worked for Congressman Jarvis since he came to Washington."

Forsman gave a moment to summarizing his notes. Then he said, "Congressman Jarvis' father is Major General Jarvis, isn't he?"

"He is."

To the other two men he said, "General Jarvis was one of the people at the Chatterton dinner last night."

Mrs. Norris bit her lip, remembering—how long ago it seemed—Tom's reading out of the paper Senator Fagan's charges. "The son isn't the father, let me tell you," she said.

Forsman looked at her curiously. "Why do you say that?"

Mrs. Norris was more cautious. "He has a bent for trouble, the old gentleman has."

Forsman nodded, pleasantly enough. "It's not necessarily trouble—I hope, though it's trouble enough for us, God knows. Do you know someone by the name of Joyce?"

"I do, or I know who she is," Mrs. Norris said, and clamped her teeth down in front of her tongue.

"Would you mind telling me . . . confidentially?"

"She's a friend of Mr. James'—Congressman Jarvis'—and a world-famous sculptress."

"Ah-h-h."

"And it was her the Frenchman took home from the Ball when Tom and I started to follow him."

"Now I've got a couple of things in place," Forsman said. "I can tell you one thing, your Irishman's safe. He's with Senator Chisholm and this Mrs. Joyce."

Mrs. Norris dumped her chin on her breast. "Trust him to that," she said.

"They all seem to have gone looking for you."

"Did they find me?"

"No, but I shall see that they do before long." He turned to the other investigators. "Senator Chisholm was also at the dinner party. Also Ambassador and Mrs. Cru."

"We don't have to check them out, do we—foreign nationals?"

"Only if they ask it," Forsman said.

"Let's get out of here before they do," Mulrooney said.

"Man, you've just begun to work," Forsman said. "But in this case it looks as though we've flushed a swan instead of duck, doesn't it?"

The men nodded agreement.

Forsman picked up the rolls of film which had made up the package Mrs. Norris found in the tree.

"Why can't I just go and put that back in the tree," she said, "and get something I left in its place?"

Forsman looked at her. "Don't you think these things should be processed so we can see what's in them?"

"That," Mrs. Norris said, "is your business. But it would seem to me that if you wanted to snare somebody else the way you did me, it wouldn't matter what was in the box as long as you caught them with it."

"You want to put the box back where you found it?" Forsman said.

"It would clear my conscience," Mrs. Norris said.

"I have no better idea at the moment," Forsman said. "Gentlemen?"

"Isn't the whole thing off?" Mulrooney growled.

"Not where Mrs. Norris is concerned," Forsman said. "She'll wait for you in the sitting room. Won't you, ma'am?"

"What's my choice?"

"A few minutes," Forsman said soothingly, "and the boys will be at your service."

"Will they take me home?"

Forsman nodded. "Wherever you want to go."

31

The truck bearing the General and other contraband cargo rattled into Washington. The General could tell their arrival by the condition of the streets: a city of monuments and broken car springs. He was not sure he had not broken a spring or two himself on this trip. It was no escapade for a man near seventy. But at least he was out of the mountains.

In the front seat, the mountain boys were singing, not raucously, and not harmoniously—just something to keep the driver awake. When the truck began a series of frequent turns, the General girded his loins, and if ever loins needed girding, his were they. He also divested himself of the striped sweater and tucked it between the cases.

As soon as the truck stopped, the General took a leap out

through the curtains, his body sinking almost to the ground as his knees collapsed. He had to hang onto the truck. Meanwhile, the sounds from within the Club Sentimentale suggested that more than one set of knees in this vicinity should be out of joint. The General did a few gingerly bends, hanging on still to the ropes.

The mountain boys were standing beside the cab door, getting their own legs and bearings.

"Hey, Red, do you hear that? And ain't it near crowing time?"

"It's past crowing time, man, and that be a chicken you're listening to, not a rooster. Matter of fact, I'd say it be an old hen."

"Sure can cackle, can't she?"

The General grinned to himself. He was safe on safe ground now. That would be Maria Candido touching up a bawdy song. He staggered around the side of the truck.

One of the mountaineers nudged the other. "Oh-oh, Red, here's one flew the coop."

"Can you gentlemen direct me to the Club Sentimentale?"

"Reckon if you got this far you ought to be able to make it there, mister."

Amen, the General thought.

"Yonder door." Red gave a nod toward the carriage lamp-lighted entry.

"Thank you very much," the General said, and did a bit of weaving on his way which was not entirely put on.

"Looks a mite like Grandpa, don't he?"

"Mite. Grandpa always wanted one of them monkey suits

he got on. I've been thinking, Red, we could afford to get him one."

"What for—to sit and rock in?"

"He'd have it to sit and rock in—or else to lie and roll in."

The General turned around and motioned to them. "Come on in, fellows, I'll stand you a drink."

"Thanks, mister, but my brother and me don't drink."

"That's what I like," the General said, "good, upstanding young Americans."

"We're Virginians, sir!"

"Bravo!" the General said, and went indoors.

No one saw him arrive. The place was dark as a cavern and misted with smoke. He had not heard a racket like this since the war's end, and he could tell by some indefinable quality to the odd ends of conversations, the pitch of voices, the air of all night abandon that there were newspaper men all over the place. So much the better, he thought.

The first thing he did was explore the back walls of the building. It was on the river's edge, he knew, but he wanted to see just where the mountain boys were going to unload their dew. He found a window at the end of the check room, overlooking the river. Even as he was looking out, one of the boys passed close by the window. It meant there was a walk alongside the building.

The General then went to the men's room to repair the ravages of a night on a bald mountain, or, to put it another way, he thought, grimacing at the face in the mirror, a bald night on a mountain.

32

"Quite a hideaway, this," Jimmie said as he drove zigzag up a mountainside.

Dolores agreed: "Leo liked to come here, he said, so's he could communicate with his soul. That doesn't sound right, communicate, does it?"

"I think it sounds fine in the context of Leo," Jimmie said. "I don't doubt he had trouble sometimes, communicating with himself."

"I'm sleepy," Dolores said.

From the high part of the mountain they could see the beginnings of dawn even as the General had seen it not so very long before.

"We're just about there," Dolores said. "Those lights—
that's the cabin."

Jimmie put out his car headlights and, not having more
than a few hundred yards to go, decided to park the car. "We
won't do any talking now, Dolores, and when we get to the
point of talking, I'll do it for both of us."

"You're welcome," she said. "I'd just as soon curl up in the
car here and go to sleep." She drew her knees up under her
and tucked her head down on her shoulder. "I'm a pussy cat.
Night-night."

Well, Jimmie thought, she might have said "'Bye now."
Everybody else was saying it these days. He took the keys of
the car with him. "All right," he said, "if that's the way you
want it, it's all right with me. But you're not to come after me
once I've gone inside."

"Bye now," she said.

Jimmie stayed in the shadows, approaching the building,
but the moon was under a cloud. It was now the darkest hour.
He was very close to it when he saw the Jaguar parked next to
the cabin. In fact, he heard the creaks and sighs of it, the motor
still hot, before he saw the automobile.

He felt squeamish about entering without knocking, presuming he could get in. Then he remembered where the Jaguar had
been in the last hour and he put his hand on the doorknob with
no further qualm. The door was unlocked. The place was aglow
with lights. Nobody here worried about electric bills, certainly.
It passed through his mind then that he had not seen an electric
light for miles. No wonder at almost four in the morning.

194

He could hear the splash of running water. Someone was taking a shower. Jimmie swore softly, as, he was sure, no man had ever sworn at his own father. He moved through the completely modernized cabin step by cautious step. He observed the arsenal over the mantel, and saw the racks that were empty, but behind which ever so faintly the shape of two pistols showed in the faded varnish of the wood panelling.

He glanced about the room then, and saw the purse, the furs, the shoes on the chair nearest the bathroom door. All the perfumes of Arabia, all the waters of Niagara . . .

Then he noticed the huddled shape on the sofa, and said with deep though muted fervour, "You old reprobate." But he moved quickly to the side of the couch, intending to rouse the sleeper. In the instant he put his hand down, he realized the shape was a dummy.

"Father?" he said in a loud whisper, for he got the uncanny feeling that the old gentleman was watching him. But the only sound was the gush of water, then a rattling of pipes as the shower was turned off. Jimmie cast his eye about quickly for a place to conceal himself at least long enough to appraise the situation. He started for the closet in too sudden haste, his foot catching the carpet and noisily tumbling an ashtray.

A few seconds later the bathroom door opened an inch or two. "Ransom, are you awake, honey?"

Jimmie groaned almost involuntarily.

"It's almost time for you to go down home, but I just didn't have the heart to wake you. Sleeping like a baby . . . no conscience, nothing. I'll slip into something and you can get in here if you want to . . ."

Jimmie backed his way gingerly to a wing chair on the other side of the sofa. It concealed him from her view unless, of course, she came to look in it directly.

"There," she said, coming into the room. "I must've fallen asleep myself. Ransom?"

Jimmie could hear the clack of her slippers and then the few cushioned steps on the carpet until she reached the couch. He braced himself to act at the moment of her discovery. It came with a little "oh."

Jimmie, speaking to her back, said, "A friend of yours, Miss Allan?"

She started at his voice and whirled around, but she had quite controlled her expression when she faced him. Life would hold very few surprises for her, he thought.

"I don't suppose you are either—a friend of mine," she said, not precisely answering his question. "May I see your identification?"

"Do you say that to all your visitors?" Jimmie said.

"Very amusing. Who are you?"

"James Ransom Jarvis, in search of my father."

"Oh." She took a towel from around her head and shook out the wheaten hair. "I don't know where your father's gone to, Mr. Jarvis. He got just awful drunk and I couldn't get him to go down home so I went to bed myself and left him here—tucked in like that almost." She made a helpless gesture toward the sofa.

Jimmie nodded and waited.

"This isn't my place really," she started up again, compelled now to tell a story, and a damned good improviser, Jimmie thought. "And I hope nothing's happened to him. I wouldn't want any scandal."

"Why did you bring him here in the first place?" Jimmie said.

She looked him in the eye. "You are kidding, aren't you, Junior?"

Jimmie could feel himself blushing from the roots of his hair. "I am very definitely not kidding, Miss Allan. I didn't ask you why he came. I asked why you brought him."

She shrugged. "That's what I thought you said. But I don't think it's fitting, you asking a lady to answer that question. And I'd be much obliged if you'd just find him and take the both of you out of here before I get into trouble."

"Get dressed, Miss Allan. You're coming with me. I think you are in trouble."

"I don't want to go, and I'll have you arrested if you try to make me."

"You're coming down to answer the charge of murder."

She opened wide her eyes in a show of innocence. "I don't know what you're saying at all. Just how did you get in here in the first place?"

"I followed the Jaguar which my father was *not* driving."

"I suppose, being so holy, you got wings."

And indeed, Jimmie knew he would have needed wings to keep pace as that car had set it. He did not answer, but instead, crossed the room directly to the telephone where it hung just inside the kitchen door.

Virginia Allan merely stood, twisting the towel idly. She had nerves stronger by far than his, Jimmie thought.

The operator came sleepily to his persistent signal. "Give me the District of Columbia Police Headquarters." He called Washington although jurisdiction was probably Virginia: let the police decide.

"Papa's going to be in a lot of trouble, Junior," Virginia said. "After all, I guess he did manage to get down there somehow without waking me up. I was expecting to make him coffee after I took the shower to wake myself up."

It was something to think about, Jimmie mused, for he supposed his father must have done just that—got back to the city somehow.

"You're even going to prove I was here all the time, breaking in on me like you did," Virginia went on persuasively.

Jimmie thought he should have brought the youngster in as witness. He should have had her with him to touch the hood of the Jaguar and be able to testify to its heat. He did not know of anyone else who had seen the Jaguar in Washington. The Key Bridge had been deserted while he examined Montaigne's body. Father and son: he sickened at the thought of what giving testimony in a case like this was going to mean.

Jimmie finally got an answer on the phone. He identified himself to the desk officer, and then said, "I want to report a violent death. The body is at the foot of the embankment on the Arlington side of the Key Bridge." He did not take his eyes from Virginia Allan while he spoke. She listened, her head on the side, her lips pursed in a little pout of mock sorrow.

"I'll be at the Club Sentimentale on K Street and the river when your men want to talk to me," Jimmie went on quickly, hoping thereby to avoid the question of where he was calling from. "The dead man's name is Montaigne. He runs the club."

"Congressman, you better stay . . ."

Jimmie hung up the phone. The call might well be checked, of course. But there was a chance that it might not, his having identified himself, and he might thus have the opportunity to offer his explanation on a saner, safer plane.

"You know Leo challenged your father to a duel, don't you?" Virginia said.

"So I've heard. And hoped to get a great splurge of publicity thereby. Why?"

Virginia shrugged. "Leo loved the limelight."

"How did you get him into the Jaguar with you? Weren't you supposed to be up here entertaining Father?"

"Honey, you don't want to ask me those questions. Look up there—" She pointed to the wall where the guns were missing. "I'm just noticing two duelling pistols missing. Leo must've taken them—or else your father did. You don't suppose Leo was shot with one of them?"

"Come on, Virginia, I've got a date with the police." He strode to the chair and gathered her purse and her furs and threw them at her. Her purse was not heavy enough to carry even one duelling pistol, he thought, but it was far from empty. "And so have you."

"I'm coming with you," she said, "but just so's I can give testimony against your father."

"I'm sure he'll appreciate it," Jimmie said.

Virginia dressed in front of him and Jimmie thought it was the only thing in her manner that told of uncertainty, for beneath the silks, the props showed: she was the sagging relic of what once must have been the fine shape of a woman. Her face had held up, but she was nostalgia from the neck down.

"Funny, Ransom didn't tell me about you," she said, putting her head through a sweater which brought back certain illusions.

"Would it have mattered?"

"I don't suppose. But I like to know about people and their families, never really having one myself." She got another purse from the drawer and was about to change her things into it.

"Take the one you had," Jimmie said.

She shrugged. "It doesn't match. But then I don't guess most things do tonight."

They went through the house together when she was ready, turning off the lights. Outdoors she turned the key in the door, and stood back a moment and looked at the cabin. "All gone boom," she said.

Jimmie was almost touched, and for the first time tonight surely.

"Going to leave his car here?" she asked.

"He can come for it at his convenience."

"Remember the Dusenberg?" Virginia said. "Leo always wanted one. I wish he could have had it."

Something was happening to her, Jimmie thought, remorse . . . Whatever it was, he counted on the confrontation with Dolores to crack her control. But her manner did not change.

"Poor little lamb," she said, "trying to be a black sheep. I don't mind sitting in the back alone."

"Sit in front," Jimmie said. "Dolores, it will be better if you get in the back. I'm sorry if it's cold there."

The sullen youngster did as he had asked.

"There's lots of places it gets cold along toward morning," Virginia said, and climbed into the front seat.

Jimmie, rounding the car, was half prepared to face some small pocket weapon, but her hands were folded in her lap and she had deliberately placed the purse where he could reach it as easily as she could.

Jimmie was troubled as he drove toward the city. Certain things had seemed to have come quite clear to him: for instance, he was sure that Virginia had been used to decoy the General, to keep him safely out of Washington while the duel was ballyhooed to the reporters. It did not matter to Leo if it all fell flat afterwards; indeed he must have expected that to happen. Jimmie also reasoned that Leo was Senator Fagan's informant; it occurred to him that Leo with his entrée to high places and high level conversations would have little trouble in manufacturing "security risks" and Virginia would have been the perfect helpmate—especially with someone like the General.

But the murder of Leo Montaigne: there was the phone call from which he did not return to the club room, and his departure within a half-hour or so, apparently telling no one in the club. Virginia had come down to see him on some pretext that was sufficient to lure him into the car with her, something presumably that could not be passed between them on the telephone, and something urgent enough in Leo's terms to justify her leaving the General alone, something that could not wait until morning. It was fair to surmise her bait to have been "security" stuff she had got out of the General. Whether or not she got it—and Jimmie suspected there was nothing his father had to give of that nature—was unimportant to Virginia. It was a tale sufficient to lure Leo.

Jimmie did not doubt at all that she had killed him. And from the moment of finding the body, he had suspected jealousy as motive; the young lover's betrayal of an ageing mistress, and the opportunity to get away with it, placing the appearance of guilt upon the General. But from the moment she turned the key in the cabin door, something in this line of conjecture seemed out of joint.

He turned his head when he spoke to her. "Miss Allan, why do you think my father might have killed Montaigne?"

It was Dolores who responded, crying out: "You said she killed him!"

"I said I thought she was implicated," Jimmie said.

Beside him, Virginia did not answer. Instead she lifted her chin and raised her voice—high, clear, and sterile as the night wind—and sang at its top, *The Old Rugged Cross*.

Jimmie could feel the crawl of his flesh into goose-bumps.

33

Tom was driven directly to the home of Senator Fagan, and on the way he resolutely kept his mouth shut. He was onto the likes of these boys, apprentices to fame. There was not a word he would let out of his mouth now wouldn't get to the senator ahead of Tom, aye, and maybe instead of him. It was a terrible commentary on human nature that the greater the man, the greedier his watchdogs.

It was a modest house, the senator's, and a great disappointment to Tom who had somehow hoped to find it cluttered with books and papers and legalistic scrolls; he had thought perhaps to find a collection of scientific instruments that would enable the senator to read beneath the lines. But the place was as neat as an old maid's hope chest.

The senator himself, however, was waiting for him in the study. He sat, bleak-faced and red-eyed, in robe and pyjamas behind his desk. He offered Tom a limp, wet hand without rising, and much to Tom's chagrin there wafted up between them the distinct aroma of whisky. Ah, but sure, it could have been mouthwash. Hadn't he wakened the man in the middle of the night?

"Now, young man, the first thing I want is the name of the general."

"Well, you see, sir . . ."

"The name of the general," one of the senator's boys said.

"I work for the son of General Ransom Jarvis," Tom said.

"Is that the man you spoke of on the phone?"

"It is."

Tom glanced up at the senator's echo. He was slowly nodding his head. And so was the senator, with that famous stubborn grin now breaking through the granite.

"Sit down, lad, and tell the whole story in your own way. Would you like a cigar?" The senator indicated the gold humidor on his desk: more gold had gone into its making than ever Tom had seen in a piece, and the handles on either side of it were the graven heads of Texas steers.

"No, thank you, sir. I have one I'll save for later."

Tom told the story as straight as ever he was likely to tell one, and while the General's part was obviously a disappointment to Fagan, he was very happy indeed with the revelation on d'Inde, since d'Inde, too, had been at the Chatterton party.

"You've done a fine turn for your country tonight, my boy,"

the senator said. He looked up at the echo. "Get somebody from the *Herald* on the phone, somebody worth talking to."

Tom was impressed with the efficiency of the senator's assistant. If Congressman Jarvis showed a little more authority, in fact, Tom's own efficiency could be stepped up. He thought for the second or two he was out of the limelight, how the boss would fit in a role like Fagan's. Sure, he had the background for it, New York district attorney at one time. And he had guts, and patriotism, sure as much as the next man; he was a war veteran. Ah, but he was shy, if you came right down to it: he wasn't the sort to light up the sky. In fact, Tom was sure, if it had been Congressman Jarvis he had taken this story to about d'Inde, he would have done the same thing as the two women: he'd have gone to the FBI, and never a word in the papers of his own part in it. Tom was convinced that good works should be proclaimed aloud; leave the whispering quiet to spies and traitors.

"Do you come from Ireland, my boy?" the senator interrupted Tom's reverie.

"I do, sir," Tom said, and told him the town.

"Do you know my grandmother came not far from there? A grand woman."

The senator's assistant hung up the phone: "Every reporter in town is at Montaigne's place, Senator. They say something's going to break there any minute."

"Get my clothes," the senator said, rising. "Get them now!"

34

The General came out of the washroom feeling much refreshed, and the more he saw of the characters gathered in The Sentimentale, all in varying stages of dilapidation, the more he thought a night in the mountains had something to recommend it.

It was only the melancholy drunks, however, that clung to the bar, ministered to by one blonde barmaid. The General had had enough of blonde maids for the night. "What's the celebration?" he asked of anyone who might give him an answer.

"Drinks on the house. All you need is a press card," a fellow of rubbery status said.

It made the General a little dizzy to watch him. "I suspected that. Is our host getting married?"

"Ha! Mañana maybe. He's challenged some old geezer to a duel. We're all going out to the battleground as soon as it comes daylight."

"Swords or pistols?"

"You're a pistol yourself. Hey, blondie, give my friend here a drink."

The General scowled and held up his hand. "Not before breakfast, thank you." He went to the clubroom and looked in: Babel could not have been worse. There, presumably, people tried to understand one another and couldn't. Here nobody was listening . . . except him, and the philosophic melancholics who were listening to themselves.

Madame Cru was dancing the Charleston, and her little pomposity of a husband was ladling out bromides as only a persistent bore could. Poor Madame, she must cherish naughty thoughts behind those shuttered eyes of hers. And it was a desperate woman who could do the Charleston at her age at four-thirty in the morning. Somebody brought Joshua Katz a violin and thrust it upon him. Katz, waltzing around her with the grace of a hippo, played out the dance for Madame.

Away went Maria Candido then, running up and down a cadenza. By God, the General admired her; she was sober enough to put words to whatever there was left in her of tune:

"Hi diddle-diddle, Katz and the fiddle,
    Ho-ho-ho—Katz and the fiddle,
    He-he-he—Katz and the fiddle,

And the cow jumped over the moon.

    Ho-ho-ho—Katz and the fiddle,

    He-he-he—Katz and the fiddle,

The little dog laughed. . . ."

Katz, very calmly and deliberately then, and with more delicacy than he had played the instrument, lifted the fiddle to his lips and then high into the air and brought it down on the coloratura's head. She swooned away into the arms of the ambassador.

The General stepped out of the doorway and went to the phone booth. He had to come out again and borrow a dime from his pal at the bar.

The reporter followed him to the booth. "Say, chum, you didn't kidnap a lady tonight, did you?"

"Have you seen one tonight you'd like to kidnap?" the General growled and pulled the phone booth door closed between them. He popped it open again. "Could you make it two dimes, friend?"

35

"The first thing want to do," Mrs. Norris said to Mulrooney, "is return the bicycle, and I'd as soon do it before I have to make any explanations."

"Madam, your theft of a bicycle is not the concern of the Federal Bureau of Investigation," Mulrooney said.

"I was thinking of you as a gentleman," she said.

"Al," Mulrooney said with a deep sigh, "drive up to Georgetown first." To Mrs. Norris he said, "Have you any notion whatever the trouble and expense your playing detective has cost the United States government?"

Mrs. Norris thought for a moment. "I shouldn't think your salary would be more than ten thousand a year. Or do you get overtime for something like tonight?"

"Never mind," Mulrooney said. "Al! Can't you drive any faster?"

"There's some sort of accident up ahead, it looks like," the man driving said. "Or maybe it's on the bridge."

"The Key Bridge?" Mrs. Norris asked.

"That's the one," Mulrooney said.

Mrs. Norris felt her stomach turn. Even as they drove nearer the bridge she could hear sirens wailing the approach of more police. The driver gave his own siren a turn just to show his authority. He pulled up to one of the troopers who had waved them down with his flashlight.

"What's happened?" Al asked, and identified himself.

"Fella murdered down under on the other side."

Mrs. Norris groaned and came very near to fainting for the first time in her life.

"Do they know who he is?"

"I don't know if it's true or not, but I heard he runs some private club a few blocks from here. Name's Fantana, Fontaigne, something like that. Blasted at close range."

"Thanks," Al said, and rolled up his window.

Mrs. Norris breathed deeply of what fresh air she could get. She and Mulrooney sat side by side the rest of the way to the house without saying a word.

"This is it, isn't it?" Al said, slowing down.

"Yep," Mulrooney said, "I can see the bicycle there against the house."

"Mr. Mulrooney," Mrs. Norris said, as he was about to step out of the car. "What was the name of that man who was killed?"

"Fontaigne. I've been thinking about it myself. Al, did you see Forsman's list of that dinner party? I'm pretty damned sure that name was on it."

The driver merely whistled.

"Would you mind waiting one minute for me?" Mrs. Norris said. "I want to run into the kitchen and I'll be right back."

"I'll run in with you then and be sure," Mulrooney said. To his partner he said, "Can you load the bicycle while we're gone?"

Mrs. Norris could hear the telephone ringing within the house while she fumbled for her key. But her fingers were stiff, near as stiff as her heart, she thought, and by the time she got the door opened and reached it, the phone had stopped ringing. "If he needed me now," she said, "I'll never forgive myself."

"Say now," Mulrooney said, following her through the dimly lighted house, "isn't that where the duel was going to be you told us about, under the Key Bridge?"

Mrs. Norris nodded assent for she could not find the use of her voice. She looked all about the kitchen table and then on the phone stand, but the card was nowhere to be found. Ah, but she knew without seeing it whose name it bore. And there on the porcelain-topped table, in her own writing, were the words still telling of where the challenger would wait.

"Mrs. Norris," Mulrooney said, and with a certain kindness in his voice, "the man that was shot—it was at close range, so it was not in a duel."

"I didn't think it was, but it's a curious set of circumstances all the same. And I'd give a great deal to know where Mr. James is right now."

"Come along now and let's get this chore over with, and maybe we'll be able to help you locate him."

Mrs. Norris looked up at him and nodded approvingly. "You have a Gaelic heart after all, Mr. Mulrooney."

36

It was Chatterton himself who opened the door to Helene and Senator Chisholm; the atmosphere as severe as a February funeral. "We've been expecting you," Chatterton said, and when Helene murmured her regrets at being present, a stranger, he smiled slightly and added, "We are all strangers to one another tonight, Mrs. Joyce, which rather proclaims you a welcome, doesn't it?"

"You're very gracious," Helene murmured, and followed with the senator as he led them into a library where a fire glowed in the grate.

Mrs. Chatterton looked round at them, and then leaned back. "I thought it might be the FBI man."

"I understand Luke Forsman will be right along," Senator Chisholm said.

Helene was introduced to Mrs. Chatterton and Secretary Jennings of the presidential cabinet. Secretary Jennings sat as rigidly erect as one in a pattern, Helene thought, stayed and corseted, soul and body.

It was Elizabeth Jennings who spoke first: "I am very sorry, Senator Chisholm, that you have been involved."

The senator looked at her in mute surprise, for the presidential assistant had spoken as though it were her fault.

Chatterton said, "I don't believe we should talk about this affair until Forsman arrives."

"Poor Edward," Mrs. Chatterton said. "Poor everybody." She sat and plucked little bits of nothing—or so it seemed to Helene—from the arm of the chair. Suddenly she said, as though she had lost contact with the present difficulty: "I wonder what they're doing at the club right now."

A moment or two later Forsman arrived, along with another agent whom he introduced, but whose name Helene did not catch, and with them was Henri d'Inde.

Chatterton said, "Now if we had Ransom with us, we should have reconvened all the respectable members of our little party."

"I resent that very much, Edward," his wife said.

"I wonder if you have any idea, Laura," he said quietly, "how much I resent it, myself."

"So we meet again so soon," d'Inde said to Helene. "Your congressman has a very zealous household, shall we say?"

"And patriotic."

"You are disillusioned in me?"

"I am confused," Helene said.

"Would it simplify matters if I now tell you the truth? I am what they call counterespionage."

Senator Chisholm, standing nearby and purposely eavesdropping, said, "What?"

"Alas, all the volunteer patriots—they have ruined my usefulness, according to Mr. Forsman, that is, and I suppose he knows what he is talking about."

The senator looked from him to Forsman who was himself awaiting Mrs. Chatterton's response to something he had asked her. He nodded confirmation of d'Inde's account of himself.

"Alas, also," the Frenchman added, "it has very much complicated my life."

"I should think it would simplify it," Helene said, "now that you can be yourself. What are you, by the way, curator or conjurer?"

"I am glad you can make a joke at this hour, *mon cher*. It will be the major decision of my life, which I am hereafter."

"Hold on one minute here," the senator said. "Just what were those photostats you were trying to get me to take a look at the other day on the Hill?"

D'Inde laughed. "Those were the theories on hydraulics and on the flight of birds, as computed by Leonardo da Vinci maybe five hundred years ago."

"That Renaissance painter?" The senator gave an off-and-on smirk in imitation of the Mona Lisa.

"That's the one," d'Inde said. "My purpose was to see if

215

someone with—shall I say?—a glancing knowledge of the mathematical sciences, would know those computations from top secret matter on short observation. Also, they were to be further reduced on microfilm: what you call a decoy. That's what I was hoping to lure a contact with tonight."

"It's a good thing I've only had a glancing knowledge of several things till now," the senator said dryly.

"All right, ladies and gentlemen," Forsman said, "we must try to be quick about this. There is very little time left. I assume everyone here wishes to make a deposition? Frankly, I think now that those could wait until daylight . . . in view of certain recent developments."

"Recent?" Chatterton said.

"Within the hour. Secretary Chatterton, who compiled your guest list?"

The secretary deferred to his wife. "Laura?"

"I did . . . but I was restricted in it. Oh, what nonsense not to tell it! Edward felt it would be to his advantage in the department to have as our guest, Secretary Jennings. Madam Jennings has all but withdrawn from social functions, and, well, she turned down my invitation.

"Afterwards I mentioned it to a mutual acquaintance—to a young man. To Leo Montaigne. He prevailed upon Secretary Jennings to come, and then suggested—perhaps I must use a stronger word—insisted that he compile the guest list. Truly, it was all of his choosing, every name on it."

"Everyone?" Forsman said.

"I believe so. It was happily true for Edward's sake, or so I thought at the time, that General Jarvis was included. He is an old friend of Edward's."

"Most likely why he was included," Chatterton said. "But with the exception of the present company, I should say it was a fairly ghastly arrangement . . . Forgive me, Laura, if some of them chanced to be your friends . . . but I do believe that in their selection Montaigne was perpetrating some monstrous joke he assumed would have been amusing twenty-five years ago, by including the singers and that clown Katz."

"And so it would have been—not monstrous, but very funny—if it weren't for these dreadful times, and that man, Fagan."

"There are other dreadful things that have happened in the last twenty-five years, Laura," her husband said, "which in their way, perhaps account for the likes of Fagan."

"Don't you think I know?" she cried out, rising from the chair. "Do you think I would have needed Leo if I didn't know? This world is too terrible! I won't live in it. I won't!"

Her husband went to her then and put his arm about her. "It's the only world we've got, Laura."

Forsman left them and turned to Elizabeth Jennings. "Madam Secretary, is there anything you wish to say to me now? You may give your deposition in private, of course."

She said with great dignity: "I think not, for the moment, publicly or privately. In the end, one can betray only oneself, and betraying oneself, everybody. I think, however, you must talk with my nephew—with the boy who calls himself Montaigne."

"I would like very much to do that," Forsman said, "but I

was informed by radio on my way here that Montaigne is dead. He was murdered sometime this morning."

No one in the room said anything, but Helene, watching Secretary Jennings, thought that the corners of her sad, firm mouth twisted downwards in a brief, ironic smile.

"I have promised the police every co-operation," Forsman said, "so we had better go together from here to where the others of your last night's guests are being detained."

37

The General, stepping out of the phone booth, became aware of the presence of several men even more sober than himself. Two of them were at the bar, one was outside the washroom door and one at the booth whom he had at first presumed to be waiting to make a call. Nobody would be abroad coldly sober at this hour unless he were getting paid for it, he decided. Therefore, he assumed them to be police.

He stood up at the bar beside his friend the reporter. "Who are they?"

"Society for the prevention of cruelty to generals. They have just announced there's not going to be any duel."

Ah, yes. The General understood now: Montaigne had

claimed to challenge him and had then taken the precaution of having Virginia detain him in the mountains. What a cheap, despicable publicity stunt! He put his hand to the letters he had stolen from a thieving blackmailer, and was more than ever gratified to have them.

"I could have told you that some time ago," he said.

The reporter turned and looked him up and down. "Then I was right! You're old han'some Ransom himself."

"I am General Jarvis, and I'm going to get out of here right now and I'd advise you to do the same thing."

The reporter shook his head. "I'm sorry, General, we're quarantined."

"What do you mean by that?"

"Those boys are really Federal Bureau of Investigation, and they say we've got to stay here till they let us go. For my part, I've passed my capacity. Every drink I take from now on, I'll get soberer and soberer. General Jarvis, sir, how about a little scoop for the Washington *Inquirer*? We didn't get a smell of last night's handout."

"My heart overflows. What was last night's handout? I seem to have missed it myself."

"Well, there's this United States senator, he's the biggest Red-hunter since Wild Bill Hickock." He then filled in the legend of Fagan's charges about the Chatterton party.

General Jarvis really could feel nothing but amusement. No doubt, there was something sulphurous going to come out of this, but he had a few sticks of dynamite of his own, if he could just set them off on time. It would be a hell of a note, however, to blow himself up, too.

The club door flung open, and somebody shouted for more light in the place. One of the FBI men shot the beam of his flashlight into the faces of the newcomers.

Senator Fagan himself had arrived, flanked by two strapping youths, one of whom the General would swear he had seen somewhere before. The other one knocked the light from the hand of the man who had shone it in the senator's face. As fast as a bullet he got a fist in his eye that would close out the light there for a week. The senator stepped over him. He had observed the presence of the press.

"Well, boys, it's not often you beat me to a story! Let's make it tit for tat. What's going on here?"

Tom was pulling on Fagan's coat-tail. Fagan turned on him: "I've got an ear, haven't I? Come up to it!"

Tom whispered, "That's General Jarvis standing at the bar, sir."

"General Jarvis?" Fagan repeated aloud.

The General stood to attention and saluted. And thus was he standing when the entire Chatterton party arrived. They were accompanied by several uniformed police, and there was not a smile to be pinched from one among them. The officers opened a corridor through the reporters into the main club-room, and the reporters closed in behind them.

"My God," the General's friend said, "you don't suppose they went through a looking glass?"

"No," the General said, "but I'm beginning to think we need a turnstile."

Senator Fagan catapulted himself into the clubroom after the Chatterton crowd. "One minute!" he cried. "A point of personal privilege!" Then at the top of his voice: "Doesn't anybody here know who I am?"

The General rubbed his hands together and, as though it were a genie's signal, the outer door swung open again. This time it was something unexpected, unexpected at least in dimension: a woman with one child in her arms and enough of them hanging on her skirts to play ring-around-a-rosie!

"The doct-err!" she demanded of the General and his friend, now the sole occupants of the bar. "I want to see Doct-err d'Inde."

"Madam," the newspaperman said, "the doctor is in the next room, but there are a few patients ahead of you."

"I am Madame d'Inde," she said haughtily and herded the brood through the doorway. The reporter and the General moved close enough to follow what was going on.

A District of Columbia police captain was standing on the orchestra dais, his arms folded and the scowl of a Cromwell on his brow as he looked down upon the mélange. His men moved among the tables and soon put the spare ones against the wall, and they silenced the giddy as they went. In truth, a pall had soon fallen over the room.

"Which one of you is Congressman Jarvis?"

There followed a few seconds of silence. "I work for him, sure, sir!" Tom cried out.

"His father's present," General Jarvis said from the doorway. "General Jarvis here."

Many a head twisted round at that pronouncement.

The policeman said very coldly, "I want to see the man who reported Montaigne's murder."

And that took the wind out of even the General.

38

"So the young man is dead! What price patriotism? All the officers of the law are amongst you, but Montaigne is dead!" Senator Fagan went forward as he spoke. The room was hushed, even to the d'Inde children who had corralled their father.

"Murder most foul! I cry it to the heavens! No wonder the people have lost confidence in their government."

"Senator Fagan," the captain said then, and severely.

But Fagan snapped at him, "I have the floor, sir. I tell you I will not see this day spent, I will not allow this collection of rogues and rummies dispersed until we have got to the bottom of this dastardly deed . . ."

General Jarvis had never seen Fagan in action. It was a

pity, he thought, that he could not now enjoy it. He knew in his bones that if Jimmie were involved, he had become so in his father's interests. It was touching and tedious, this dogged devotion, and it made him infinitely sad that he was unlikely ever again to be able to run away from home.

"Let it be known now," Fagan continued in resonant eloquence, "Leo Montaigne was in my employ. He volunteered his services as truly as a soldier. And he has died by an assassin's hand. The country will not be safe until he is avenged. I demand protection for my people . . ."

No one was really surprised by Senator Fagan's information, and having at hand such intimate letters as were in his pocket, the General doubted not that Montaigne had numerous sources of confidential information. And God knows, Fagan had an insatiable appetite.

The captain of police made another feeble attempt at interruption, only to be brushed off by Fagan. He could hold the devil at bay, this man, and possibly he thought he was doing just that. It would be the unresolved question of a decade.

The General edged his way through to where Mrs. Joyce was standing. "Do you know where Jimmie is?"

"I have no idea," she said.

"Is he saving me again?"

She nodded, smiling a little.

"I think it would be better this time," the General murmured, "if he would save himself. I have had certain obligations fall to me this day. Excuse me, my dear."

He moved on to the side of Madam Jennings. Her face was

225

as grey as the morning sky before sunrise. A new commotion by the bar-room door created a distraction. The senator had to strive for attention. But the General was glad of the disorder: there was even, it seemed, some little good in bedlam.

"Madam Jennings," he said, leaning close to her ear, "I have managed, almost by inadvertence—and not much courage, I'm afraid—to rescue a certain property of yours. There are some letters in a package I shall give you now, six of them, I believe. I assure you, Madam, I have read no more of them than told me they were yours, and perhaps made me wish they had been addressed to me." He bowed ever so slightly and put the envelope into her hands.

She did not look at him, did not speak, merely clutched the letters. A few seconds later her eyes were welling with tears that she did not attempt to conceal. But she was still looking straight ahead.

Madame Cru, a few paces away, glanced in their direction, and seeing the flow of tears, ungushed her own. Maria Candido put her head on poor old Katz' bosom and wept unrestrainedly. The General was waiting for the wails to start.

They did, but from another quarter: d'Inde was being besieged by d'Artagnan the magician's wife—and children. The General started to count, for the place was swarming with kids. He gave up counting at eleven, knowing he had missed some. Doubtless, they totalled twice seven.

Even Senator Fagan yielded. "You, you, sir . . ." He pointed at d'Inde, for Tom was whispering in the senator's ear. "Somebody arrest that man. He's a spy."

"I am a counter-spy!" d'Inde shouted.

"I don't care what kind of a spy you are! Arrest him!"

"Hold everything," Forsman said, trying to take over on behalf of sanity. "He *was* a counter agent, Senator. But he's taken this double-life business far too seriously for us."

A newspaper reporter broke in: "Only two lives to live for his country! What a television gimmick!"

"Television?" Senator Fagan said. "Did someone say television?"

The police officer, in desperation, took his whistle from his pocket and blew it: it quieted the house.

"Has anyone here any information on where Congressman Jarvis might be? You may as well understand, you're not leaving until he is found."

"I've been waiting for you to get to me, Captain," Jimmie said from the doorway.

The General cried, "My boy!" and pushed back through the mainstream to where Jimmie and Virginia Allan were standing hand in hand, reluctantly hand in hand. No one really noticed the sulky Dolores whom Jimmie had hold of with his other hand.

39

"Ransom, honey," Virginia said, disengaging herself from Jimmie who gave her to his father's care, "your son is a brute. And you never even told me about him."

"It's something a woman has to find out about a man for herself," he said.

Jimmie said, "Hold her for your life, Father." Then he raised his voice: "Who is the officer in charge?"

"In charge of what?" someone quipped.

"The investigation of Montaigne's murder," Jimmie said, "since I should think in this case the last thing comes first."

"I am," the captain of police said.

"Technically," Fagan added.

"All right, Senator," the policeman said angrily, "Let's get technical."

Jimmie said, "I charge Miss Virginia Allan with the shooting of Leo Montaigne, and I am prepared to give evidence substantiating the charge."

"The first thing I want," the captain said, coming up, "is the weapon."

Virginia, defiant as though the cause were far from lost, said, "Okay, Congressman, give it to him. He wants the weapon."

Jimmie said, "Father, open Miss Allan's purse."

"With your permission," the General said to her, and took the purse from her hands. She gave it willingly enough.

"No weapon, Jimmie," the General said.

"Her gloves, may I have them please?"

Grey kid, they were, and rather soiled for so dainty a female, spotted as though a child had pencil-dotted them, and even as he gave them into Jimmie's hand he could smell the gunpowder on them.

Jimmie, without a word of explanation, lifted them to his nose and then handed them to the officer in charge. He did the same thing. Then he turned to her.

"I arrest you, Miss Allan, on suspicion of murder."

It was very simple, said and done, and a certain awe hung over the room at the dreadfulness of the moment after all. Even the murder of a rogue connived against the living.

"Don't you want to know why?" Virginia said. And she moved with that old grace and sway that had made the

229

Club Sentimentale a gaudy tribute to the good old days; she moved, unrestrained, to the middle of the room. Why not, the General thought. Everyone was doing single turns, as the vaudevillians called it. "Leo was washing me out. I made him, and I unmade him, because of that little Miss Dolores Nobody. You know, friends, and I got some here I like to think, Leo was a bad person."

"Enough, woman!" Fagan cried. "You're speaking of the dead."

"Honey," and surely it was the first time he had been so addressed since infancy, "I ought to know that better than you even. But I'm going to say out now something I don't even think you know. Whatever Leo promised you about four people at that dinner last night, he was going to make it up, him and me. I did most anything for him. Even up to the end. I lured that dear old gentleman—General Jarvis—out of town for him—and I came back in and told Leo all about him and the Russians . . ."

The senator moistened his lips and interrupted, "What did you tell him, Miss Allan?"

Virginia smiled. "I told him General Jarvis knew how to count in Russian."

The dear old gentleman was beginning to feel cantankerous; he did not feel old and he certainly did not feel dear.

"That's all I told him, but you see, I had to tell him something to get him into the car with me. And it was all so easy then. I used the duelling pistol, and I just thought it was all going to look like the General did it, him being a fighting type man. But I'm a softy. I thought he was asleep and in the end I was going to swear he stayed up in that cabin until after dawn, and I hoped he'd do the same about me. You're going to have to drag the Potomac River to find those pistols. They were a pair, but I only used one. I shoot true."

The General, if he had not felt cantankerous, would have been tempted to a certain sentimentality himself. Virginia had begun to sniffle, and she had won more than small sympathy. Jimmie was no doubt thinking what she would be like on the witness stand. He would not want to be the prosecutor. But then, Jimmie never really wanted to be a prosecutor. It was why he had escaped into politics. If the General were going to feel sentimental, it was better at the moment to feel it about his son.

"Dear Ransom," she said, and with a gesture from the heart stretching her hand toward him, "Would you fetch me a hankie from my purse?"

The General had been sent to the well once too often. He brought Virginia the handkerchief she asked for, but he held the purse still and when he turned his back to her, he drew from it a large white envelope and, with the flap open, drew from it the papers inside.

Senator Fagan, with the eye of a falcon, pounced across the room ready to collect any documents.

The General, however, lifted his guard and warded off the gentleman. He read the top line aloud:

"Never sally when you can dally . . ."

Tom let out an agonized shriek: "That's my poem! I wrote it myself to a girl in Ireland!"

231

The General handed over the sheaf of poems to their owner. "Young man, you need never fear being plagiarized."

"But, but . . ." Tom turned and spread out his arms to Jimmie. "Boss, I gave them this afternoon—or yesterday, whenever that was—to Mrs. Norris to read. Will you tell me what they're doing with this wench? I'd never have asked her to read them, sure."

"Tom," Jimmie said coldly, "where is Mrs. Norris?"

"If I knew, sir," Tom said quite humbly, "I don't think I'd be here now."

Luke Forsman stepped up to them then and said, "I think it's safe to suppose she is home by now—having spent a night quite as wild as anyone else here." He looked Virginia Allan up and down. "If you had been picked up in the park in Arlington tonight, Miss—would it have prevented you from committing murder?"

She shook her head, and this time that fair head was bowed.

Forsman went on, addressing himself now to Tom: "Mrs. Norris, when she got tired waiting for you, picked up our plant—you see, the two of you got in the way of a prearranged contact between our agent and the foreign courier. We thought months of work was undone till now . . ." He turned and nodded at the General, by way of tribute.

"Then you might say I discovered a spy!" Tom cried, unwilling to let go fame when it was so near.

"Well, possibly uncovered," the Federal man said.

"My boy!" Senator Fagan said, and laid his arm across Tom's shoulder.

Jimmie spoke up then: "Well, since you put it that way, Senator, you can have him." He went to Virginia and took her hand, much as a lawyer, which he was after all, might take a witness' leading her to the stand.

"Since we've come this far together, Virginia, why not tell us now the real reason you murdered Montaigne?"

"He knew," she said quietly. "He saw me a week ago with the man . . . who pays me . . . the Big Man, and he recognized him. Leo never forgot anything or anybody, and he'd met him in Europe and knew what side he was on. I was one of the four names he'd promised to Senator Fagan, and then my whole life, love and adventure was all over."

"Who were the others?" the senator asked. "I demand you tell me their names now. You will be protected—the best lawyers . . ."

Jimmie realized in an instant that not one name had yet been given to the newspapers—nay, not even to Fagan. He had released the Chatterton story on Montaigne's promise.

"Aren't you going to arrest this woman?" Jimmie said, catching Forsman by the arm and inspiring him to haste.

"I arrest you, Miss Virginia Allan . . ." Forsman started.

"She's already under arrest," the police captain shouted.

"And I demand . . ." cried Fagan over all.

And not one of them ever finished the particular sentence he had started, for at that moment, another breeze swept into the place, and somebody shouted, "Quiet!" Four men stood abreast just inside the door. One of them stepped forward and waved his credentials over his head. "Nobody try to leave! Everybody in the house is under arrest. This is a Treasury Department raid."

"What for?" somebody shouted.

"For the sale and consumption of illegal alcohol."

General Jarvis chuckled. He had indeed got caught in his own explosion. He had promised on the phone to sign the complaint, but he hadn't actually done it yet. It wouldn't matter, though. They were here, and so was the stuff. They would find out for themselves, having a search warrant. But they might in time have to wash out the arrests.

"Look here," Forsman cried, going up to the Treasury officer, "I'm a Federal agent myself."

"Then more's the shame on you, getting caught!"

Suddenly then, one of the women screamed.

The place was tilting one way, then another.

"An earthquake!" someone screamed.

A good, hearty voice spoke out: Senator Chisholm: "It's an act of God, and high time."

Jimmie knew well the feeling. So did the General: he had been to sea oftener than many a sailor.

"No real cause for alarm!" Jimmie said, cupping his hands over his mouth. "Nothing to be afraid of. This place was built on a barge. Somebody's cut us loose, that's all."

There were some sensible people aboard, or perhaps they were merely exhausted. They stood where they were while those closest to the windows broke open the shutters. And by the dawn's early light, they were indeed sailing down the river, slowly, ponderously, but inevitably.

"Who's at the helm?"

"There is no helm, madam."

"Then what's to become of us?"

"It would seem we are now to have our chance at immortality," the General said.

Jimmie reached Helene's side. "Don't be alarmed, darling."

"I assume there are two possibilities," Helene said, "either we sink or we float, and right now, Jimmie, I don't think I'd know the difference."

The weight of the barge broke their last contact with land—the lights went out.

And in the phone booth, one reporter was cut off from his night editor just in time to save his job.

40

Mrs. Norris, Mulrooney and partner could not find a place to park, so crowded was the neighbourhood with police and government cars, and then finally, leaving the car half-blocking the street, they were almost run down by a canvas-topped truck.

Mulrooney shouted the driver down. "Where the hell do you think you're going at that speed?"

"We're a-going home, man, fast as we can get there. We got work to do."

"Where's home?"

"Yonder mountains, friend."

"By the looks of that thing you're driving," Mulrooney said, "you'd better stay there."

"Man, you never gave better advice in your life. We don't ever expect to come down again."

"Where's the Club Sentimentale? Do you know that?"

The red-headed man grinned. "I understand it just moved out of drydock. It now a-floating perty as a bar of soap."

The two investigators and Mrs. Norris walked zigzag through the cars and down to the water's edge even as the sound of the truck echoed over the hollow. A bit of song hung in the air after them and then it, too, faded away toward the far hills: "Wake up, wake up, darling Cory. What makes you sleep so sound? The revenue officer's a-comin' to tear that still house down . . ."

The Club Sentimentale was almost midstream, easing toward Theodore Roosevelt Island. Mulrooney examined the hacked ropes and shore lines, the severed pilings. A moment later a public service truck arrived, its crew ordering them to stay right where they were until the power wires were safe.

"We'd have been here for whatever happened," Mulrooney said, "if it hadn't been for you misplacing the tree."

"A tree is a tree is a tree," Mrs. Norris said, "except that it's not by moonlight." A nip of sun was peeking over the horizon. "Isn't it lovely to waken the sun?"

"I'd rather any day it wakened me," Mulrooney said.

Mrs. Norris contemplated the quiet, floating barge and the gentle river, all as peaceful as a Scottish sabbath. "I wonder," she said, "if there is anyone aboard it."

About the Author

Dorothy Salisbury Davis is a Grand Master of the Mystery Writers of America, and a recipient of lifetime achievement awards from Bouchercon and Malice Domestic. The author of seventeen crime novels, including the Mrs. Norris Mysteries and the Julie Hayes Mysteries; three historical novels; and numerous short stories; she has served as president of the Mystery Writers of America and is a founder of Sisters in Crime.

Born in Chicago in 1916, she grew up on farms in Wisconsin and Illinois and graduated from college into the Great Depression. She found employment as a magic-show promoter, which took her to small towns all over the country, and subsequently worked on the WPA Writers Project in advertising and industrial relations. During World War II, she directed the benefits program of a major meatpacking company for its more than eighty thousand employees in military service. She was married for forty-seven years to the late Harry Davis, an actor, with whom she traveled abroad extensively. She currently lives in Palisades, New York.

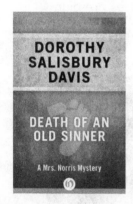
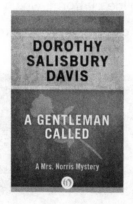
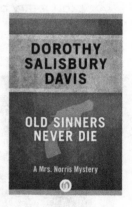

OPEN ROAD
INTEGRATED MEDIA

Open Road Integrated Media is a digital publisher and multimedia content company. Open Road creates connections between authors and their audiences by marketing its ebooks through a new proprietary online platform, which uses premium video content and social media.

CPSIA information can be obtained
at www.ICGtesting.com
Printed in the USA
JSHW021407270623
43855JS00001B/73

9 781480 460430